Rhiannon Owens

To t
Thanks so much for all
your support!
Rhiannon Owens
Ashley O'Keefe.

Rhianno

&

Asley

Ashley O'Keefe

Independently Published

Contents

WINTER & CHRISTMAS   *34*

Foreword

I first encountered Rhiannon and Ashley around a year ago when I became aware of a new book they'd both collaborated on entitled, 'A Voyage of Poetic Discoveries' (Rhianno & Asley Poetry Collections: Book 1). The pair had previously met online, during the pandemic via a local creative writing group. Something clicked between them as they developed a mutual appreciation of one another's poems. Ashley's poetry really spoke to Rhiannon and vice versa. Then came the idea to publish a book of poetry together. Eventually their dream became a reality as they saw their new creation in print. Both were delighted to view copies of their book on the shelves at various local libraries and in some retail outlets too.

Their writing styles are very different, but in many ways they share some common ground in the stories they wish to convey and the word pictures they enjoy painting with one another. Rhiannon mainly writes poetry but enjoys writing short stories and monologues too. Ashley has completed his first feature film screenplay and is half-way through writing a second.

After reading their first collection of poems, I was blown away by their writing styles and how they complement one another as poets, and I suppose you could say: compliment one another too! I was delighted to discover both had read my book, The Workhouse Waif. I was impressed with the way the story helped to inspire Ashley's imagination as he then went on to pen several poems based on scenes from my story. I was really impressed how a story originally from the creative recesses of my mind inspired him to write those particular poems, which were highly lauded and commented about on social media! Rhiannon, too, has had much acclamation online for her poetry as her poems spring to life from the page with a sensual symmetry which is sometimes soft and sometimes surprising, but never stale.

Rhiannon and Ashley's poetry has a dreamlike quality for me as they paint pictures with their words and bring their poetry to life from the page, leaving the reader thinking about their poems long after they've been read. Since that time they encountered one another online during the pandemic, the pair have gone on to meet one another several times in person and have also collaborated on further poetry books, this being their fifth together!

I hope you'll enjoy their selection of poems as much as I have. This really is a lovely book to have on your coffee table, to dip in and out of as you wish when you have a quiet, reflective moment in your day to spare. I think we are going to see a lot more from this talented duo in the future and I, for one, look forward to it with fervour.

Lynette Rees
(Author of The Workhouse Waif)
https://www.facebook.com/authorlynetterees

Introducing the Authors

Rhiannon and Ashley 'met' via the Merthyr Tydfil online Writing Group in 2019... and finally met out in the real world in 2021! This is their fifth joint poetry book to date!

The 'Rhianno & Asley' series came about due to a misspelling of Ashley's name. Rhiannon wrote a poem about a monster called Asley, and Ashley responded with a piece about a rhinoceros called Rhianno...

This creative partnership is built on respect and a mutual appreciation of each other's work. Their writing styles are different but complementary, and they have become firm friends.

Rhiannon and Ashley have been featured in promotional spotlights for the Dark Poetry Society, and were thrilled to be interviewed by well-known Merthyr author, Lynette Rees. They both have work published in anthologies: 'Quintessence,' the 'Merthyr, They Wrote' series, and the Ravencage and DPS e-zines (including the recent print versions).

Their books can now be found in Merthyr and Caerphilly libraries, South Wales, as well as in a number of independent bookstores such as The Hours (Brecon), Cover To Cover (Mumbles) and Theatre Soar in Merthyr.

Both continue to pursue their individual writing projects, but you can rest assured that the Rhianno & Asley Voyage isn't over just yet…

Follow their journey on Facebook:

https://www.facebook.com/RhiannoAsleyPoetry/

Rhianno & Asley...

Rhianno *(Part 5)*

Rhianno stands proud
Rhianno stands strong,
Rhianno lives on
And on and on...

Rhianno's face smiles
Yet her sad eyes show,
She remembers back
To the waterhole,

Now a little slower
Wrinkled with pain,
Remembering the day
She fought back the rain,

She dreams of her lover
In dreams, they connect,
Those nights of passion
She will never forget,

Rhianno stands proud
Rhianno stands strong,
Rhianno lives on
And on and on...

Ashley O'Keefe

Asley *(Part 5):* **A Reckoning?**

"I am Asley, I rule all...
in my inferno mankind falls...
I AM ASLEY!"

Asley's eyes crack open
as the earth rumbles and tears
erupting with sores,
he's on his haunches
"I'm ASLEY!" he roars,

but a beast stands before him,
a beast who has him dwarfed,
Asley shudders, struck dumb
"Who...?"
but the Titan only laughs...

"I was born of your own vile hatred of course!"

Asley thunders,
Asley roars...
ashes float silently like rain
as he crouches, defensively now
cowering on the floor,

The beast has him frozen,
this beast spews frigid ice
and Asley is paralysed
as his torso is ripped and sliced,

He cannot fight
he is unable to flame,
this creature of his hate
renders him immobile...
again and again...

but then there's a glow up
up in the sky,
Asley's bloodshot eyes
gaze, staring
itching and dry,

At a phosphorescent being of golden radiance
who cries...

'I am all the good you destroyed - I am Life
I am Love
I am Compassion
I am Beauty,

and so much more...'

Asley roars and roars
but what is this?
Could it be
tears,
upon mighty Asley's cheek?

Real salt tears that rain down,
that pour?

Does he sink down to the floor,
or does he stand tall?
Coming back more venomous
more hateful than before?

Is this his redemption or just his final downfall?

"I am ASLEY..."

Rhiannon Owens

Art of Expression

*A show of feelings
through many external signs
inspires emotions*

The Tango

Sensual and short
Revealing clothes,
Intricate fringes
Her cleavage shows,

His straight-cut trousers
Shirt and shoes,
Her high heels poised
The dance ensues,

The 'nuevo tango'
Begins to play,
The 'tango accordion'
And violin sway,

In a close embrace
Her hand on his hip,
Held in the crook of his arm
Her head back slick,

Movement of body
Movement of feet,
Timing, speed
The rhythmic beat,

Leader and follower
Embrace, intertwine,
It's raw, it's sexual
Impulsive, sublime,

Combining with sharp turns
Step to back, to front, to side,
Crossing and flexing

On the floor, they can't hide,

Swinging her leg
Hooking it around,
The boleo, the gancho
Her partner it's found,

Movement of body
Twirl and glide,
Movement of feet
Slip and slide,

Sophisticated patterns
So intense,
Vibrant and playful
Erotic elegance,

Combining with sharp turns
Step to back, to front, to side,
Crossing and flexing
On the floor, they can't hide,

Swinging her leg
Hooking it around,
The boleo, the gancho
Her partner it's found,

Fascinating, sensual
Synchronised romance,
A dialogue of limbs
Caress each other as they dance,

A moving seduction
Across the floor,
Intriguing, asymmetrical,

3

Sexual and raw,

Combining with sharp turns
Step to back, to front, to side,
Crossing and flexing
On the floor, they can't hide,

Swinging her leg
Hooking it around,
The boleo, the gancho
Her partner it's found,

Leading her around
Curving the floor,
In dramatic style
Their erotic encore.

Ashley O'Keefe

Duende (The Soul of Flamenco)

The guitarist sets the tonality
punctured with falseta interludes,
melodies of descending tendency.

Songs of longing and desire,
lamenting voices,
almost an ululation of pain.

An emotional intensity,
this fire and passion
sweeping the audience up
in a whirlwind,
clapping, singing along
caught in a frenzied tempest.

The dancer with her proud carriage,
arms move with expressive flair
as she stamps rhythmically across the floor,
fiery and tempestuous
in swirls of dizzying red,
as the tempo builds and builds
and builds
its powerful staccato beat,
heading to its crescendo
in a whirling, sizzling, smouldering
flurry of arms, legs, grace, sweat,
ecstatic
release…

Rhiannon Owens

A Stare Without a Smile

QUICKLY...

The people gather
To this place where they've been led,

SLOWLY...

A shirt glides up and over
His intelligent, confident head,

Beneath, a rippling torso
Not a drop of perspiration,

He limbers up in readiness
To the crowd's anticipation,

In his spiritual dimension
Of self-discipline and belief,
An art of concentration
Lightly jogging on his feet,

Almost rocking like a pendulum
Ticking like a clock,
Unarmed and dangerous
Very soon he'll run amok,

With balance and accuracy
An invisible kick and punch,
With speed and agility
His opponent's bones will crunch,

EYES of concentration
A STARE without a smile,

Not many men would face him
Most would run a mile.

Ashley O'Keefe
(Inspired by Bruce Lee)

A Work of Art

There's a stunning portrait on my wall
that brings me so much pleasure
of someone so noble, of visage so pure
I stand and peruse it at my leisure.
So beautiful that personage
my eyes can't look away
I should have left the house an hour ago
but cannot tear my eyes away.
I cannot describe in words
how aesthetically pleasing it is to me
I'm hypnotised by that goddess
who reaches out to me.

With all the charms of Botticelli's Venus,
a nymph of Rubenesque curves,
graceful as a Monet
where a stream gently bubbles and swerves.

As radiant and romantic as a Pre-Raphaelite
tragic Ophelia, or Proserpine clutching forbidden fruit
as breath-taking as an Angel in the Sistine Chapel
as joyful as a Medieval painting,
all troubadours, jesters and lutes.

Skin as clear and fresh as one of Constable's skies

with Van Gogh's stars reflected in her eyes
as elegant as one of Degas's dancers,
as knowing and mysterious
as Mona Lisa's smile.

The shell of her ear
fit for a pearl earring,
as bold as Lichtenstein,
so colourful a Frida self-portrait would be dull,
I've never seen a painting so fine…

Ah, no wait hang on
that's not a portrait on my wall
it's my reflection in the mirror
that has me so enthralled.

Rhiannon Owens

Sketches

Lines of graphite on paper
Different shades of grey,
Pencil outline sketches
Unfinished drawings to convey,
A more finished picture
A painting, a golden fleece,
A completed work of art
From sketch to masterpiece.

Ashley O'Keefe

Brushstrokes

A hand moves across the canvas
Without thought, instinctively,
Creating a new painting
For all the world to see,

Imagery and reflections
The creator's creativity,
A palette of wondrous colours
Brushstrokes, so skillfully.

Ashley O'Keefe

The Perfect Painting

To create the perfect painting
To hold it in a frame,
To dream of its beauty
His desires, he'd inflame,

With an insane lust for life
In ill health and solitude,
He took himself to Paris
To paint the people nude,

Bold became his colours
So dramatic and expressive,
Such impulsive brushwork
From this man who was depressive,

Mental illness consumed him
Living in poverty and squalor,

A razor fight with Gauguin
Took the ear above his collar,

Psychotic and delusional
Torturing his suffering soul,
A brilliant, troubled mind
With nothing left to console,

Sorrow turned to Sunflowers
In a Wheatfield with the Crows,
A deafening CRACK! one Starry Night,
And like his brushstrokes, his blood flows.

A smoking revolver
On a palette painted red,
Sadly, his paintings came to life
Long after he was dead.

Ashley O'Keefe

Expression

Take my hand,
turn blinking into the daylight,
our backs to the darkness,
using our imaginations to take flight.

Under a pristine, endless blue sky
over the raging indigo belly of the sea,
leaving behind all confusion,
where we can finally think clearly,

and breathe evenly once more,
inhaling that sweet air so pure,
knowing that together we are stronger
and that we have the power to break free.

Rhiannon Owens

How My Poem Grows

A thought, an idea
Enters my head,
Who puts it there?
As I wake from my bed,

A feeling, emotion
Comes from the heart,
I have to take notice
The writing must start,

As the poem grows
The memories flood in,
Times from the past
My pen starts to sing,

Gracefully swirling
It glides across the page,
A mystical magic
An encore on stage,

Beautiful, poignant
A message of hope,
Rhythmically rhyming
Helping to cope,

A thought, an idea
Who puts it there?
I look to the skies
For my Father, my prayer.

Ashley O'Keefe

Poetry

Real poets for me
Write not just how they see
But also how they feel
Neither doggerel nor spiel
And sometimes it might lack appeal...

But it always says something
Even if layered in ambiguity
With us hesitant to peel back the layers

Even if we hate what they say
Because it contradicts our shit-eating smiles
And our 'Have a Nice Day!'

Rhiannon Owens

13

King of the World

When I write
I'm on a mountain peak,
Amongst the clouds
The words I seek,

Surveying all before me
I look around,
Across the land
There's a story I've found,

In the distance
A far-off place,
My eyes zoom in
Those writings trace,

King of the World
I share it all,
Just one cackling echo
I stumble and fall...

...But, I always get up
Dust myself down,
Climb back up that mountain
And put on that crown.

Ashley O'Keefe

The Little Sparrow

Singing from the bordello
a little sparrow blindly searches the skies
its song resonates with loss and sorrow,
chansons and ballads that bring tears to your eyes.

Living la Vie en Rose,
seeing life in rosy hues,
surviving, loving, feeling
a voice that echoes through time,
a voice that speaks of pain and of healing.

A surge of powerful, raw emotion
rousing, transporting us oh, so high,
she sings of never having regrets
with a poignancy that makes us cry.

Somewhere, an accordionist
plays for this little bird,
her song swells,
bursts forth from afar,
does she sing of lost love
to a silhouette boxing in Heaven,
amongst the moon and the stars?

Rhiannon Owens
(Inspired by the life of Edith Piaf)

Time to Mend

The last line written
A full stop at the end,
The page finally finished
Now I need time to mend.

Ashley O'Keefe

NATURE:

Across silver silk
Pearl dewdrops shine gracefully
Amid sunlight streams

Frozen Flames

Nurtured with love
By Mother Earth,
From roots to bloom
Stems from its birth,

To drink from the rain
In the sweet smell of dawn,
The soft scent of dew
From the soil, it was born,

So bright and so cheerful
Warming like the sun,
Like frozen flames
Its blaze has begun,

Yellow petal rays
Bringing happiness and joy,
Lifting our spirits
Sunflower life we enjoy.

Ashley O'Keefe

Nature's Promise

The winter
Sunshine glows
Tenderly

Frostbitten
Bare branches
Dare to dream

Of kisses
And rebirth
Come sweet spring

Rhiannon Owens

Structure

Sunlight streams
In morning haze,
Nature's wonder
Within dawn's rays,

Intricately fashioned
With silver silk,
Delicate lacework
Of this veiled ilk,

Stretching out
On a welcome breeze,
Adorned and billowing
Amongst the trees,

Dewdrops shine
From the silky thread,
Graced like pearls
On a webbing bed,

Created with
Such loving care,
Its shy creator
We see so rare.

Ashley O'Keefe

The Huntress

The huntress scuttles speedily
Across the silken strand,
To greet the prey caught in her web
Secretes her venomous gland,

Eight blackened eyes shine like pinheads
Mandibles clunk and click,
Her quarry, she wraps in a parcel
A neat bundle spun from silk.

Ashley O'Keefe

Leafcutters

These are not the soldiers
though they march for miles
carrying up to 20 times their body weight,
neither major, minor
nor minim…
these skilled workers,
the mediae,

Foraging, cutting
bringing leaf fragments back to the nest,
to all the other workers;
the soldiers and security guards,
the gardeners who tend the fungus,
the childcarers,

and,
the Queen,

the precious brood,
their society is complex
their colony is huge!

and these workers will help sustain
the lifeblood of that nest
tirelessly marching, cutting,
they never complain…
never rest!

Hundreds of them in a line
busy lifting,
hefting,
carrying…

they do their very best!

Rhiannon Owens

Flies

In aerobatic flight
On tiny wings,
With high-speed sensors
It manoeuvres and sings,

Buzzing its tune
It shuttles on by,
Landing on food
Making baby cry,

With claws and pads
They are able to cling,
To all our smooth surfaces

As they annoyingly sing.

A rolled-up newspaper
Or even my cat,
Would pounce and claw
Or make them go SPLAT!

Ashley O'Keefe

Stars

Sleep tight as stars
Twinkle bright
Above you, gleaming
Radiant, keeping you
Sweetly dreaming

Rhiannon Owens

Breathtaking (in its beauty)

Glowing across the water
A pathway meets the sun,
Breathtaking in its beauty
A golden sky outrun,

Night-time moves ever closer
The evening drawing in,
Tomorrow is a new day
And the sun again will sing.

Ashley O'Keefe

Starlit Beauty

As lovely as their daylit cousins
though not so showy or gaudy,
an elegant beauty all their own,
feathery antennae on the alert...
but here is one moth
that really stands out,
hovering alone...

Hovering
Hovering

In hues of olive and pink
with such sensitive eyes
that colours of ultraviolet,
blue and green
can be picked out in starlight,
shades of purple
and aquamarine,

Searching, seeking

Hovering
Hovering
in the lowlight,

with curled proboscis,
tasting nectar
in the deepest,
darkest hours of night,

Travelling by twilight
seduced by floral scents,
the heady notes

and honeyed waft
of honeysuckle blooms,

in dizzied pleasure he floats…

A paradise of perfume
and colour,
wings beating with the highest frequency,
under a canopy of stars
such unaffected, simple beauty,

In daylight he slumbers
as pretty butterflies flit by,
and dreams of darkness falling
when he can soar
in enchanted wonder
under that moonlit, starry sky…

Rhiannon Owens

Butterfly (Flutters)

Fluttering
fluttering…

tiny, exquisite wings

Trembling
vibrating…

with delicate quiver,

and proboscis seeking
unfurled

she flutters
from flower to flower,

in search of sweet nectar
to warm and still those wings

after she is replete,
and has given a joyful shiver

Fluttering
fluttering…

her little heart sings.

Rhiannon Owens

Breathe

Of stem and branch,
Of leaf and root,
With water and nutrients
They grow, bear fruit,

For decades, for millennia
They live, they breathe,
From them, life's oxygen
They give, we receive,

Embracing both
The earth and sky,
Roots and branches
A fresh air supply.

Ashley O`Keefe

Mother Nature

Melting our hearts
Openly wooing us
Though we rarely take note
Hearts too full
Enchanted by cheap gloss
Reality is too poignant

Never taking a moment
Always seeking the superficial
Taking time over nothing
Useless, ugly emotion
Rearing its head
Earth cries in shrink-wrapped beauty

Rhiannon Owens

Autumn's Breath

Gold and scarlet
A carpet of leaves,
Gliding, swirling
Falling from trees,

Dancing spirits
Autumn's breath,
Twirling, spinning
Summer's death,

Vibrant hues
Bold and sweet,
Autumn's beauty
Summer's beat,

Flames of foliage
Leaves pirouette,
An earthly aroma
Summer won't forget.

Ashley O'Keefe

Love Bites

The whisper in his ear sends an icy thrill quivering along his backbone. Voicing its ardour, desire. Its hunger. He shudders, waiting for the vampiric bite…

Then Mr Cwtchy gives an ear-splitting yowl as metal teeth rake across him - he doesn't know if he hates flea or flea comb more!

Rhiannon Owens

Intruder

In darkest night
In peaceful sleep,
An intruder swoops
An intruder creeps,

An open window
By sound, not sight,
A creature's wings
Flap through the night,

A sharp incision
Through human skin,

Lapping its victim's blood...
The vampire bat has been.

Ashley O'Keefe

Sleepy Dawn

As the sleepy dawn breaks
With its sweet birdsong,
A melodious chorus
Still to the night, I belong,

An indigo sky
Makes way for the blue,
As the stars disappear
Into the sun's rising view,

Stretching my body
I let out a yawn,
Lying tall in my bed
As the new day is born.

Ashley O'Keefe

Jenny Wren

Mum always said that
if our cat (Pip) killed a Jenny Wren,
she'd throw him out
(she never would have!)
but he never did catch one,
at least, not where we could see…

and now,
hark at this wren
with its cocky swagger,
puffing out dull-brown plumage
as though he's a bird of paradise!
Cheeky dip of the beak,
shake of the wing
and a tilt of the head,
then, a demonstrative flick of tail feather!

A quick preen,
a hint of mischief
dancing,
in his bright eye,
that twinkles
as he trills,
not a lilting voice,
more, a raucous laugh.

What has happened to his pretty song?
Ah, now I see…
he hops out of reach
from wall to branch
to cherry tree
and
to the wall again,

laughing at Iskra
our beautiful,
wren-pecked cat!

Rhiannon Owens

Face with no Grin

Crystal clear waters
A slow running stream,
Flows into the river
Of a pebble-bedded dream,

Sun glints on the water
Below, shafts of light,
Cut through the surface
With a hooked line for a bite,

Flexing its body
Back and forth,
Stretching, expanding
Relaxing muscles take north,

Moving it forward
With a caudal fin,
Pushing through water
A fish face with no grin.

Ashley O'Keefe

The River's Roar

Tumbling down the rocky outcrop
Hear the river's roar,
The power in its flow
From a heavy downpour,

Rushing waters lapping
Against a stony riverbed,
Between the riverbanks
Overhanging trees up ahead.

Ashley O'Keefe

A New Day

A blanket of mist
Drapes across the land,
Trees in silhouette
The mountains stand,

The loneliness
Cold and eerie,
Echoes rise and fall
Eyes are bleary,

In silence, in stillness
In the bleak early morn,
A crow cries out
A new day is born.

Ashley O'Keefe

Running with The Pack

He bays his wolf howl
this ferocious snarling beast

The pack
echo it back ...

To this pug with big dreams!

Rhiannon Owens

Secret Whispers

The rain speaks in whispers
Secrets it does tell,
Grumbling clouds striking out
Like a blinding light from hell,

Clashing, crashing, booming out
With a thunderous aggressive roar,
In a cloudy sky; overcast
The clouds cry their heavy downpour.

Ashley O'Keefe

The Wind (Gift of Life Songs)

The wind stirs
Sings its song,
Of hopes and dreams
And times long gone,

Rustling through trees
Swaying grassy wands,
Feeling emotions
In its gift of life songs,

Powerful and passionate
Gentle and fleeting,
Flowing so freely
Soothing and greeting,

Feeling its freshness
Through tousled hair,
Gusting its chorus
Singing without care.

Ashley O'Keefe

WINTER & CHRISTMAS:

*Angel shapes imprint
In the newly fallen snow,
Children's faces glow*

Choppy Waters

New Year's Eve rolled into the New Year
and conditions were bad at sea,

I realised, waking to the sound of
raucous mewling and screeching,
as seagulls swooped and soared
and fought with a bullying grace,
over leftover twixmas scraps
and over a discarded doner kebab,
the kick of chilli sauce sending them over the edge,
a squalling, squawking frenzy
of savage scavagery,
as they battled over a discarded chip
spotted from 100 yards away,
to the victor the spoils!
Rich pickings indeed
for these feathered, festive fiends,
a veritable smorgasbord of delight!

I lay in my bed
reflecting on the year just gone,
listening to the gulls...
thinking of the bad conditions at sea,

imagining the heavy grey skies
hanging ominously over the thrashing waves of the ocean,
as little boats determinedly
push onward, onward...
ever onward.

Rhiannon Owens

Silent Freeze

Frozen crystals dangle
Coldness setting in,
Fingers chilled, no longer bend
White puffs of breath rising,

A pure white desert
From near to far beyond,
Looking across the distance
Over Winter's covered pond,

In a slow silent freeze
As ice sticks to fur,
Ploughing through white powder
In my panic, it's all a blur,

The Grizzly quickly closing in
The gun frozen to my horse,
Struggling with fur mittens
It hits with ending force.

Ashley O'Keefe

Autumn's Despair

Crystals dance on Winter's breath
Heaven's glitter fills the air,
A dusting of snow covers the ground
Snowflakes frolic in Autumn's despair,

A wintry landscape
Trees clothed in white,
Rooftops drizzled
In pearly ice overnight,

A fresh new canvas
Awaits the new day,
Footprints and mittens,
Winter's here to stay.

Ashley O'Keefe

Prancing

I fling a snowball
right at you,
and push you
down
into the snow,

watch you flounder
in the powder,

then I collapse down
next to you
starfishing,

not one snow angel
but two,

brushing crystallised
diamonds
from your face,
stealing a kiss
… can you keep pace?

Laughing merrily
Ho Ho Ho!

Here we go…
prancing
dancing,

dashing through the snow!

Rhiannon Owens

Thundersnow

Blowing, swirling
A howling gale,
Vision blurred
A Winter's Tale,

Out of the blizzard
The sky aglow,
Deafening, booming
Thundersnow.

Ashley O'Keefe

A Winter Wander

Walk, breathe
and live in the moment,
in the here and now
with no worries on your mind
and nothing to make you frown,
get the blood circulating
enjoy the scenery,
enjoy nature's abundance
which remains undaunted
despite a picture that is wintry,
because red berries shine like rubies
and pine trees reach out a friendly bough,
you walk and everything
is serenity
in the frost-kissed here and now,
and when you return back home
to the bosom of your family,
you'll feel content and warm
just being with them,
surrounded by love
as the cat purrs away on your knee.

Rhiannon Owens

Bequeath

Bequeathing its leafy garland
A gift of seasons past,
At the feasting table,
Exchanging goblets for a promise made to last,

Autumn turns to Winter
The sun turns a shade of blue,
Its icy rays shining down
The cold and chill ensue,

On frozen land, Winter's cradle
Returning to Mother Earth,
A carpet of leaves and berries
The Ice Queen's jewels for rebirth.

Ashley O'Keefe

Winter (Wonderland)

Following the footprints
footprints in the snow
leading into the forest,
how far should I go?

The sky is a blizzard
of whirling white
swirling snowflakes,
footprints disappear
from sight.

All is silent,
awe-inspiring

but then such rare delight,

a tiny robin
pipes his song,
singing just for me
and puffing out
his warm red breast,
proud of his musicality.

I could stay here for hours
if Jack wasn't nipping
at my ears and nose,
there are chestnuts roasting
and snug blankets calling,
I touch the bloom of
a late flowering rose.

Making my way back
I'd come further than I thought
no breadcrumb trail to follow…
but my gentleman robin
he knows the way,
hopping ahead
his little forked prints
lead me over dips
and hollows…

Then I've left the forest
and he gives a final trill,
the warmth of home
hits my rosy cheeks,
kissing away the chill.

Rhiannon Owens

Frozen Place

Gnarled and twisted trees
Wrapped in an ethereal mist,
A place for the dead and dying
Now frosty and icy kissed,

Walking through the graveyard
Leaves melt into the ground,
Tarmac pathways meander
Like rivers of black ice without a sound,

Headstones... scattered
Strewn upon the wintry land,
I see old friends beside them
I smile, I raise my hand,

Running amongst the headstones
Four small boys laughing, having fun,
Not one coat between them
Their young souls only feel the sun,

Walking aimlessly for hours
Amongst echoes of the past,
My memories drift with time
There's a grave I face at last,

Gnarled and twisted trees
Wrapped in an ethereal mist,
Within this frozen place
I did once exist.

Ashley O'Keefe

Christmas Has Come Early

Christmas has come early
Before Halloween,
It's time to cheer ourselves up
After the year that we've just seen,

The Christmas tree lit up
Decorations all around,
We've even got the music playing
Christmas songs abound,

We never do this normally
We leave it 'til December,
But there's nothing else in lockdown life
So we're going on a bender.

Ashley O'Keefe

Baubles & Bling

Oh, Christmas tree
I gaze at you
my lips curve in a smile
for your pretty baubles cheer me up
but only for a while,

Your fickle lights
flash on and off
teasing me with promise,
I can't look away
my eyes,
shine with rapture,

I stay loving,
I stay honest…

Rhiannon Owens

Christmas Time

Christmas is a time for family
It's a time for fun,
But we really should remember
It's not for everyone,

For those who've lost their loved ones
For those all alone,
Christmas can be lonely
Better times they have known,

Christmas is a time for giving
It's a time for us to share,
A time for believing
A time for quiet prayer,

Whatever you do this Christmas
Please spare a little thought,
Always think of others
Less fortunate and distraught.

Ashley O'Keefe

Snow Angels

Little children in the snow
forming angel shapes,
sweeping arms
and legs out wide
imagining beautiful wings
that they'll create,

then parents call them in
and angel shapes glisten in snow,

while Christmas Angels
watch from up above
sprinkling glittering dust,
to soon-to-be slumbering
and sweetly dreaming,
little children below.

Rhiannon Owens

Covering of Snow

Branches bow and bend
Under a covering of snow,
Beneath, a pathway, powdered white
Footprints come and go.

Walking up The Old Line
Along the new Taff Trail,
Kicking up our heels
Where once lay sleeper and rail,

A place of childhood memories
A place of childhood friends,
A place where we made friendships
The kind that never ends.

Ashley O'Keefe

'Make the Dark Sky Bright...'

A thousand Christmas lights
lit up for me,
and more lights twinkle
on the Christmas tree,
and a star shines bright
in the winter sky,
to guide pilgrims to a manger
where a tiny baby lies,

but I feel like that star is shining
especially for me,
illuminating my hopes
sprinkling glitter on my dreams,

Christmas lights glare brightly
and Christmas bells will peal,
but you put the light into my life,
you made the good things real.

Rhiannon Owens

Scented Smells

Snow has fallen all around
Hear those jingle bells,
Blowing, rubbing, clapping hands
Mulled wine, scented smells,

Heavenly songs singing out
Faces full of joy and cheer,
Couples catching arm-in-arm
In this moment held so dear,

Trumpets, horns and those trombones
Play with lively exuberance,
Sounding out throughout the town
Lit up with wonderful luminance,

Steamy breath, wrapped up warm
We gaze into each other's eyes,
Raising our fingers to each other's mouths
We take a bite of those mince pies,

Such a clear bright starry night
Those smiles from the moon appear,
There's that magic chill in the air
Around the Christmas tree this year.

Ashley O'Keefe

Ice Sculptures

She claps her mittened hands
together in delight,
"Oh, they're so beautiful!"
she exclaims joyfully,
gazing rapturously
at dozens of sparkling
ice sculptures,
the reflected light
is diamonds
and emeralds,
topaz in her lively eyes,
"I wonder who made them?"

He shrugs,
"Who cares?"
He swigs at the vodka bottle
and grips her waist
with one meaty arm.
Enthralled by the sight before her
she wriggles impatiently,
runs a hand down the curves
of a crystal swan,
a perfect palace of glass,
so enchanting…

He grips her harder
and begins to push his hands
beneath her cloak,
and she tries to push him away,
"Stop it"...
She struggles to break free
but he's too powerful,
she tries to scream

but he clamps a hand over her mouth…
and who would hear her anyway?
His trousers are undone,
he licks his greasy lips…

Creaking
Cracking
Shattering
… An explosion of sound,
screaming…

and she is flung backwards
into the soft, powdery snow,
and all sound is swallowed
and she is blinded by light…

Silence
Silence

Shakily she clambers to her feet
and sees him, lying prone
eyes wide and surprised
and unseeing,
his body run through
with a thousand diamond shards,
a thousand razor-sharp icy kisses
stained scarlet with his blood,
glinting like so many
precious rubies…
the biggest rammed savagely
into his groin
that blooms a crimson flower,
arcing across the snow

and in front of her

a lone ice sculpture still stands,
a magnificent Angel
wings unfurled,
radiating strength
and ferocious beauty,
wielding a fiery sword
that dances,
licks
and sparks
with sapphire flames.

Rhiannon Owens

This Means War

Thwack!

A PELT, an IMPACT
A BURST of freshly fallen snow,
Showered with feathered crystals
Your face all aglow,

Walking through the snow
I just couldn't resist,
Compacting the ball
Then a flick of the wrist,

Your face full of laughter
That glint in your eye,
Tells me in that instant
'This means war and I'll die',

Chasing me around
Heels kicking snow in the air,

50

You finally catch me
And rub snow in my hair,

Falling to the ground
In each other's arms,
Rolling and laughing
Then suddenly… ALARMS,

Bells, they ring out
Our eyes say we may,
As we kiss in the snow
Our lips show the way…

… Into the warm
In front of the fire,
Wet clothing removed
A warming scene to admire,

Frozen fingers tingle
Pins and needles play,
A cold numbing feeling
On the fur rug, we lay,

Shadows are swaying
The fire crackles and sparks,
Through snow-covered windows
A neighbour's dog barks,

Chris Rea is playing
Still not home yet,
It's a night to remember
One I'll never forget.

Ashley O'Keefe

Snow is Falling, All Around (Sisters)

'It'll be lonely this Christmas...'

Phone alarm cuts cruelly
into her tortured dreams,
one moment of unthinking bliss
and then the pain, she screams,
and throws her Samsung across the room…

Timid tapping at her door and Grace
and Hope
pop wide-eyed faces around the doorframe,
"Piss offffff" roars Belle
and Hope's little face blanches as she buries it,
sobbing, into Grace's side.

Belle feels bad,
but soon she hears the two giggling,
ripping open gaily-wrapped presents in their parent's bedroom,
bitterly she reads the message from Dave
over and over again...

'Had a laugh but wiv Tina now. She more fun. Soz'

'He's gone… 2,000 miles away... I miss you...'

Belle miserably digs in the snow,
'Belle 🩶 Dave'
over and over again,
crying tears that do not freeze
because her cheeks are swollen and hot.

"You'll get cold" pipes up Hope,
 sucking on the end of one messy plait,

and she runs when Belle snarls at her,
even as the cold and wet
seeps into her jeans,
but Belle doesn't care...
she might as well die out here in the snow!

Whooompphhh...

A snowball splats into her sad face,
at 2,000 miles an hour,

Grace stands, hands on hips,
a challenge in her dark eyes...
"We need help!" she states,
gazing levelly at her sister
and pointing her thumb
at a pile of implausibly high snow,
"We can't reach to put the head on!"

Belle looks at the serious little faces
and she smiles despite herself,
heaves her sodden bum out of the slush
and helps to roll the head
into a less misshapen specimen,
then plonks it on top,
dusting off her gloves as they admire their handiwork.

"I think he needs something" she muses,
"SHE", says Grace, "She's a Snow WOMAN"...
Belle laughs and takes the cheap nasty scarf
with the stupid Christmas trees
and crap pom-poms from around her neck,
a present from Dave...

"There we go!"

Their Snow-Woman looks the biz!
Grace says "You'll get cold!"
and little Hope screws up her face,
thinking hard for a moment
and then brightens,
unwinding the mass of red tinsel
festooning her big bobble hat,
and Grace takes it and puts it across Belle's shoulders...

'There must have been some magic...'

Belle receives a message on her phone,
**'Hiya Belle, it's Chris. Sorry u can't make party. Would u like
to meet after bank hols?'**

Chris sits next to her in history and maths,
he's lovely
and makes her laugh,
she'd never thought before...

'Sounds nice. With fam at moment. Will get back 2u…

'Once bitten and twice shy...'

She pauses before sending

'Merry Xmas Chris. Xx'

They watch all the usual suspects,
Frozen,
Fools and Horses,
and Morecambe and Wise Christmas specials…

overly sentimental films,
where they all bawl away

but dad most of all!

Belle is reading a bedtime story to Hope,
and Grace is listening though she's 'not a kid anymore'...

and the phone pings once more

'You are so pretty. Xx'...

Belle smiles,
she'll send a reply tomorrow,
but right now, she has to tuck her sisters up tight.

Rhiannon Owens

Believe

The Spirit of Christmas
Lies in your heart,
Hear the bell ring
Believe... it's the start,

Giving and kindness
Happiness and joy,
It's a wonderful life
We must not destroy,

Keep the magic burning
Let little faces glow,
Keep hearing the bell
Even after we grow.

Ashley O'Keefe

A Christmas Gift

Looking out of my window
and you are standing there,
with a Christmas gift for me...

the gift is seeing you,

I press my hand against the window
and you do too
a warm spot on the glass,
my Christmas gift...

the gift is being
so close to you,

We look at each other
you see all of me,
know me
entirely
and all that is true,
a Christmas gift for me...

that Christmas gift is you,

You turn and walk away,
gone...
my final view,
a Christmas gift
but for me
an empty box...

my Christmas gift is never you...

Rhiannon Owens

Ting-A-Ling

Within your hand
A silver bell,
Listen, shake it
That magical spell,

'Ting-a-ling'
That sweet little sound,
Ringing out
A belief you have found,

The Spirit of Christmas
When you truly believe,
The happiness and joy
When you give not receive.

Ashley O'Keefe

Glitz and Glamour

Has the tree lost its beauty?
Do we need to dress it up?
In baubles and tinsel
Like an overflowing cup,
With lights that flicker
And glittery things,
On the top sits an angel
Unfurling her wings,
We make it so pretty
It was pretty before,
But for Christmas, glitz and glamour
As you walk in that door.

Ashley O'Keefe

HISTORY:

A field fell silent,
Not a bird nor song in sight,
Poppies bid goodnight

La Pasionaria!

They shall not pass, she roared
Hearts of the people soared
Eyes flash with fire, implore
You hear her passion and stand tall,

She did not speak melodiously
Her voice held no sweet musicality, but
Always vibrated with expressive sincerity,
La Pasionaria holds you enthralled
La Pasionaria leaves the crowd awed,

No Pasaran! she declared
Of the fascists, neither cowed nor scared
The spirit of the people, she fervently shared,

Passion Flower was the name given to her
Adversity had her bloom brighter, never despair
She raised the banner of Communism with flair
She was steadfast, with a strength that is rare.

No Pasaran!

Rhiannon Owens

Nothing but Blackness

Nothing...

   ... Blackness...

      ... Nothing but blackness...

Nothing but blackness
Day after day,
For weeks, months, years
For decades I pray,

Thousands of years
Maybe even more,
Nothing but blackness
Can't move, there's no door,

Suddenly, a sound
In the darkness of night,
Nothing but blackness
Then a small light,

Digging and scraping
Clearing away,
A bright blinding light
Can't see so I pray,

Above me there's movement
People all around,
With trowels, hand shovels
Picking through the ground,

Around me there are relics
About me there are bones,

Beneath this sodden earth
I lie amongst stones.

Ashley O'Keefe

Terror on the South China Seas

No, yo-ho-ho and a bottle of rum here
this is terror on the South China Sea,
for Cheng I Sao commands her fleet
and the Ocean is Mistress to She,

At the top of the pirate hierarchy
after her husband's death,
taking her 'adopted' son as a lover
before he'd barely expelled his last breath,

The pirate armada was formally arranged,
following a strict brutal code
deserters had an ear cut off,
raping female captives meant beheading
with the woman chucked overboard…
always good to lessen the load!

Protection rackets and plunder,
negotiations with European powers…

from prostitute to cresting the waves,
and finally back on dry land
running an illegal gambling house
for the rest of her days…

one final racket to pass away the hours.

Rhiannon Owens

A Field of Spring

Silently staring
Focusing in,
On crimson petals
In a field of spring,

In the mind's eye
A sunny sky darkens,
Birds stop singing
And the memory sharpens,

Barbed wire and mist
Puddles and mud,
A place of death
Where bullets scud,

The stillness, the silence
Of 'No Man's Land',
Glaring out from the trenches
Innocent eyes await the command,

Cold and dark
The damp, the gloom,
The clock is ticking
As angels loom,

Letters written
Thoughts of home,
Young men prepare
Young men alone,

The clock is ticking
The angels sigh,
Eyes fill with fear

But they don't cry,

The end they know
They anxiously wait,
For the whistle's blow
To seal their fate,

The echoes of whistles
And rapid-fire,
As those dark skies lighten
Souls cry out from the mire...

... Silently staring
Focusing in,
On crimson petals
In a field of spring.

Ashley O'Keefe

Dreams of Old

'I have a dream'...

Martin Luther King proclaimed,
and history was born...

a dream of children
playing together,
growing up in a world
free of hatred and prejudice,

'I have a dream...'

Freud liked to talk about dreams,

for him, they revealed
our deepest desires,
hidden emotions,
anxieties,
obsessions...
and within his theory,
our dreams
regardless of content
were all about releasing sexual tension...

makes you wonder of what
Freud dreamed?

Dreamcatchers were used
in some Native American cultures
to protect children from harm,
other ancient cultures
believed dreams to be
prophecy...
it was said that Ritchie Valens
dreamt of his death in a plane crash,
but two years prior to his death
a plane came down on his school,
classmates died...

were his dreams indicative
of prescience, divination, memory
or fear?

Bing Crosby dreamt of a White Christmas,
as do children across the land,
though for most
it will only be a dream,

our history and futures are forever

bound up in our dreams…
we live and dream,

'I have a dream'...

and somewhere,
another piece of history
is born.

Rhiannon Owens

First of its Kind

The heat
The steam
The mechanical torque,

The pressure
Pushing
Pistons back and forth…

The transformation
Into rotational force,

By connecting rod
And flywheel of course,

Trevithick's steam locomotive
The very first of its kind,
Hauls a train along Merthyr's tramway
Out of an inventor's engineering mind.

Ashley O'Keefe

Rocket

A Rocket in name only
huffing along the tracks…

At 12 miles per hour,
not the most elegant
nor sophisticated of its ilk
but got the job done,
proved its mettle
with its steaming, locomotive power.

Rocket,
is making a new history,
the little Stephenson loco
beat off the competition,

Huffing along
huffing along…

She alone completed the Rainhill trials,
the first intercity railway
Liverpool to Manchester,
who knew this method of transport
would transcend decades,
travelling for miles and miles.

A Rocket in name only,

Huffing along
huffing along
huffing along the tracks...

Rhiannon Owens

The Seven Arches

In the pre-war era
The high-point of the year,
An annual Sunday School outing
Was many people's summer cheer,

From their local station
Catching that Merthyr to Brecon train,
To Pontsarn they would travel
Take refreshment, then entertain,

Beneath those seven arches
The laughter and the fun,
Playing games throughout the day
Until the day was done,

Below that Pontsarn viaduct
Next to the Taf Fechan river,
A place of natural beauty
Above the Blue Pool's water giver.

Ashley O'Keefe

Jinga

A fearsome reputation,
an Angolan heroine
of shrewd negotiations
and a bloody legacy,
all fire and determination within…

Using a female slave as a chair
but as a Queen would

'never use the same chair twice,'
she had the helpless girl executed,
some kind of bloodthirsty vice?

The heart of her nephew
she is said to have devoured,
licking lips with lascivious glee,
murdering her own flesh and blood
feasting on her own family,

There was talk of cannibalism
and infanticide,
ancient, gory rituals
all designed
to strengthen the tribe,

Keeping company with mercenaries,
fond of male attire
draped in rich animal skins,
eyes flashing fire,

Skilled with sword, axe and bow,
at her disposal a harem of men
(and she did dispose of many),
for her formidable appetites
to be satisfied again…
and again,

Ever the warrior, right till the end
buried with bow and arrow in hand,
this magnificent and terrible elderly lady,
ruler of these lands,

Was Jinga ruthless and cruel?
Has she been caricatured as savage

by white European men?...
What is truth and what is fiction?
That she was a woman
of legendary renown,
is one fact we can state
with conviction.

Rhiannon Owens

On Old Battlefields

On old battlefields, proud
Standing tall and defiant,
Crimson poems bloom
Through sun and rain, silent,

Words for the fallen
Words for the brave,
Words for the living
Words for the grave,

On old battlefields, proud
Standing tall and defiant,
Crimson poems grow
Standing tall like a giant,

Words of the sacrifice
Words that we weep,
Words of the hope
Their eternal sleep,

On old battlefields, proud
Standing tall and defiant,
Crimson poems stand

Our young men, face the tyrant,

Words of the fallen
Words of the lost,
Words of the winning
Words... at what cost?

Ashley O'Keefe

The Brown Bomber

Born in Alabama,
in a ramshackle dwelling place
destined to be a great fighter,
everyone would know his face.

Breaking down colour barriers
in golf, as well as boxing ring,
mocked as being an 'Uncle Tom'
but any progress in a bigoted world,
can only be a positive thing.

Opponents such as Max Baer,
and the 'Tonypandy Terror'
Tommy Farr,
he never gloated over the defeated
always gracious,
which helped cement him as a star.

With Max Schmeling
there was a legendary rivalry,
the two of them used as pawns
for their respective countries,
propaganda for or against Nazism

two men pressured into
becoming enemies forsworn.

One of the greatest punchers of all time,
he earned his place in history,
the powerhouse they call 'the Brown Bomber,'
the champion,
the one and only
Joe Louis!

Rhiannon Owens

Resting in Ruins

Standing high on a hill
Of natural limestone,
Upon an iron age hillfort
A castle was grown,

Looking over a river
The Taf Fechan; the 'Great Stream',
So that's how they named it
'Mawr Glais' (Morlais) Castle, with esteem,

A defendable escarpment
Built by Gilbert De Clare,
Overlooking Brecknockshire
To extend control from his lair,

Now resting in ruins
Debris from towers with a crypt,
Dismantled with time
Its stones have been stripped,

But still a great view
In those distant skylines,
And as the sun rises
On its battlements, it shines.

Ashley O'Keefe

Rock of Ages

Yes, I'm just a rock
of little interest to you,
remnant of a crumbling castle
that was so imposing,
long ago
but oh, the history in these walls,
the stories I could tell you
of War, Betrayal,
Love
and Treason.

Yes, I'm just a rock
but perhaps I'm sedimentary
with many layers
contained within me,
evidence of my origin
from a time you cannot even envisage,
far before I was quarried,
and fossilised life forms
swirl deep inside me,
alien to you
but a testament to my longevity.

Yes, I'm just a rock
passively jutting out of

this grassy hillock,
where you and your
pretty girlfriend
speak of love...

Well... she wasn't speaking so much
when I saw her yesterday,
your girlfriend,
she was far too busy
with your best mate,

but what I saw
couldn't possibly
be of interest to you,

because I'm just a rock...

Rhiannon Owens

The Place of Barking Hounds

A castellated mansion
Commanding a great scene,
Of valley and of ironworks
Crawshay's rags and riches scheme,

Cyfarthfa, 'the place of barking'
Where hunting dogs were heard,
The home of ironmasters
In a place; molten metal stirred,

Every evening from its windows
A glow, a wondrous sight,
Across the way, those ironworks

Lit up the darkest night,

The pounding and the clanking
The flame of furnace roar,
The billowing smoke from chimney stacks
The masters wanting more.

Ashley O'Keefe
(Cyfarthfa loosely translates from Welsh as 'the place of barking' as hunting dogs were regularly heard in this area of the town).

Daughters of Sparta

Trained in gymnastics and athletics
to maximise their fitness and beauty,
skilled in the art of war
and able to run wild, swift and free.

A scandal the talk of Greece,
these women not confined to the home,
spending their days in wrestling and sport,
bare limbs taut in loose attire
as through forests and hills they'd roam.

Fathers, lock up your daughters!
Husbands, where are your wives?
Have your women-folk heard tell
of the free women of Sparta?
Do they burn with the desire
to live their own lives?

Rhiannon Owens

The Runner's Heart

Inhaling… exhaling…
Inhaling… exhaling…
Inhaling… exhaling…

Feet pounding the ground
Heart pounding the chest,
Panting, heavy breathing
A true stamina test,

But first…

Let me take you back
To the very start,
To the birth of Griffiths Morgan
Those first beats of his heart,

From the small village of Llwyncelyn
To the farm called Nyth Brân,
He would run with his sheep
In the fields from boy to man,

Nyth Brân meaning Crow's Nest
Griffiths took the name on,
Now known as Guto Nyth Brân
Griffiths Crow's Nest, he'd become,

They say…

His speed was first noticed
When he was a boy,
He chased and caught a wild hare
To his Father's overjoy,

Running to Pontypridd Town
He wouldn't let his tea spoil,
Running back the seven miles
Before his Mother's kettle could boil,

Feet pounding the ground
Heart pounding the chest,
Panting, heavy breathing
A true stamina test,

Seeing his potential
The local shopkeeper, Sian,
Soon became his trainer
And much more in his barn,

She organised his first race
Against an unbeaten English Captain,
On that Hirwaun common
An Englishman's ego would flatten,

Guto kept on winning
His betting spectators getting richer,
More wealthy, more joyful
Their faces such a picture,

Life was so good
Guto and Sian were in love,
Unbeaten, now thirty
Their lives hand in glove,

It was time to retire
Time to settle down,
Spend time with his family
As rich faces turn to frown,

With several years now passed
A new champion had emerged,
Called the 'Prince of Bedwas'
With a reputation for a late surge,

A smug look on his face
His smirk could be seen,
As he boasted boldly
"I'm the best that there's been!"

With pressure from his followers
And that look in Sian's eye,
Guto took up the bait
Deciding once more to fly,

One last run for a thousand guineas
But with little time to train,
The race was set for twelve miles
Over Newport and Bedwas terrain,

Inhaling… exhaling…
Inhaling… exhaling…
Inhaling… exhaling…

Feet pounding the ground
Heart pounding the chest,
Panting, heavy breathing
A true stamina test,

Now nearing the finish line
The 'Prince' held a slender lead,
One final lung-bursting effort
And Guto's heart finds the speed,

Such a joyous celebration

Collapsing into his beloved's arms,
With his final heartbeat
He smiles and whispers…

Ashley O'Keefe
(Inspired by Griffiths Morgan 1700-1737, better known as Guto Nyth Brân,
'The fastest man of his time').
Thanks to Helen Protheroe and Gareth Roberts for the idea.

Chorus of Sighs

A prisoner drinks in the beauty of Venice
for one final time,
the tears are bittersweet
as they gather at the corners of his eyes,
he has no regrets he tells himself,
but knows this to be a lie
as he gazes through the window of the bridge,
gazing out from the Bridge of Sighs...

The lovers are enjoying Venice,
such vibrant beauty on which to feast their eyes,
soft lips seek welcoming mouth,
fingers secretly caress thighs
and they smile at the wonder of it all,
those feelings that surge and rise
as a gondola trails the water under this bridge,
beneath the Bridge of Sighs...

Rhiannon Owens

UNREQUITED LOVE:

Only Dreaming

I dream about you
the whole night through, but a dream
is all it can be....

Star

Every night I wish
upon a twinkling star
wondering if you think of me,
as I do of you...

Saying a prayer,
wishing you were near
but you are always distant,
will never bridge the gap,
it's too wide, too far...

Twinkle Twinkle,
can't you dream of me too?
Believe, just as I do?
I wish I may, I wish I might...

I'm wishing on a star,
Please, dream
a little dream
of me tonight.

Your lips dust kisses on my eyelids,
as I slumber deep, I sleep tight
but it isn't your mouth I can feel,
though my sweetest dreams
say it is so,

It is just the soft strokes of the moonlight
that illuminates the gentle blush
suffusing my soft cheek,
a lover's blissful
tell-tale glow.

Perhaps you'll see my little star,
twinkling just for you,
and know that each night
we make love in my dreams,
no matter where you really are
or with who...

Rhiannon Owens

Soulful Glow

Beauty is your heart
It's all that you are,
You're Heaven's warmth
A shining little star,
With your soulful glow
You mesmerise,
The smile on your face
Yet there's sadness in your eyes,
If only you could see
What your life could be,
You'd smile with those eyes
And life's truth you will see.

Ashley O'Keefe

Unrequited

I'm thinking of you all the time
Wishing I could make you mine
To touch your face
To feel you inside
An explosion of desire
As we wildly ride
How do you taste?
I imagine how you sound
How you smell
It's more than lust
But I can't ever tell
Each day I fall a little deeper
Than before
But you stand oblivious
Don't notice me
Don't stumble at all
And that makes me fall further
Than I ever have before

Rhiannon Owens

You'll Never Know

My heart is longing
It's longing for you,
The pain, the hurt
I'm broken, you're glue,

Standing at a crossroads
Rain starts to fall,
Which way to you?

I wait for your call,

But it never comes
And you never show,
My heart is breaking
And you'll never know.

Ashley O'Keefe

Realisation

Thinking of something you said
Then I realise,
That there's a grin splitting my face
From ear-to-ear,

Then that small realisation
Makes my heart begin to race,
Thoughts spilling unbidden into my head
Imagining your dear, sweet face,
Where have these feelings come from?
Why does my heart clench so?
With a resonating pain that sears?

How do I make them stop?
All the feelings, the longing?
I never even realised they'd appeared.

Rhiannon Owens

Fun

The clock seems to miss a tick
as my heart misses a beat,
time stops,
no ticking, no beating,
no words.

I've turned into a statue,
your face is stone,
my heart full of fissures,
yours a swinging brick
pounding it to dust.

Your words ricochet around my head,
'It's been fun,
but that's all it was,'
(shrugs shoulders)
'Just a bit of fun!'

Now the clock ticks again
and my heart stutters in time,
like a distorted Beach Boys record
as your words echo
in the emptiness of my hopes
and darkest recesses of my mind...

Fun
Fun
Fun...

Rhiannon Owens

Longing Heart

My longing heart
Watches you leave,
After years of commitment
Alone I must grieve,
Dying inside
A hundred deaths,
I'm numb, I'm drowning
Gasping for breaths,
There is so much left
To remind me of you,
In those quiet moments...
My heart calls to you.

Ashley O'Keefe

North Star

My little star
tries hard to be brave,
but be sensitive
handle with care,

It is so often eclipsed,
outshone
by bigger,
brighter stars,

(Look for it,
there!
Past the Big Dipper,
a northern star)

My star isn't much
to shout about,
a flicker,
a glimmer,
a tear in my eye...
a smudge in the inkwell
of a swirling,
indigo
starry sky...

but it is a shard
of my crying heart
that twinkles
and glints
solely for you...
seen by many
but for your eyes only.

Rhiannon Owens

Silent Song (Different Shores)

The silent song of love
A shining star in night's sky,
Longing, hoping, wishing
Yet too far to reach, we sigh,

Gazing from a distance
Discretely from different shores,
At its wonders and its magic
Which could be mine and yours.

Ashley O'Keefe

First Star You See Tonight

You think you've lost sight of the little North star,
but she's always here
shimmering, vibrating
with emotion,
never gone very far...

For all the others are not
pale imitations,
in a sky black as tar
but just polished reflections
of your hopefully watching
vivacious and loving
Little North Star!

Rhiannon Owens

Without You to Hold

I've been lying awake for a couple of hours,
Can't stop listening to those wonderful showers,
The wind blows the rain on my windowpane,
The night is cold without you to hold.

I've been watching you for quite some time,
I hope one day that you'll be mine,
I need you so and I want you to know,
The night is cold without you to hold.

Those Midnight showers keep on falling,
But it's your voice I hear calling,
Those Midnight winds keep on blowing,
But it's my heart I feel flowing.

I've got to ask your name one night,
I've seen your smile, your eyes so bright,
I'll keep you warm, out of the storm,
The night is cold without you to hold.

Ashley O'Keefe

I Want You to Be Happy

I want you to be happy
so I should set you free
knowing as I do
that you aren't in love with me.

I should let you go
it isn't fair on you

I want you to be happy
because my love for you is true.

My heart is full of you
I want you to be happy
if I set you free
won't you come back to me?

I want you to be happy
together we can be great
but you just won't accept it
you're a weak, snivelling ingrate.

I want you to be happy
the towels and blankets are cosy
the pipes in the airing cupboard are warm
so… why should I set you free?

I want you to be happy
that's why the chain's so loose
I feed and water you well
so, why not just enjoy my love?

… You're being an awfully silly goose!

I'll bake you super cookies
put rollers in my hair
clean the cupboard every day
bring fresh-cooked meals in tupperware.

You don't need your freedom
I'll never let you go
I want to make you happy
we're meant to be you know.

Rhiannon Owens

Throw Me a Line

Suffocation…
Drowning in a sea of love,

Reaching my hand out to you
Won't you take it,
Knowing deep down in my heart
we can make it.

Desolation…
Drifting further out to sea,

Calling out your name
Don't you hear me,
Waving my arms in the air
Can't you see me,

Throw me a line
I'm sinking in pain,
Throw me a line
Slipping away,
Night after night
Day after day,
Slowly drifting further away.

Condemnation…
Rowing over stormy seas,

Dreaming of you
How it ought to be,
Sailing along
on an open sea.

Ashley O'Keefe

90

Lips Meet

Our first kiss…
I remember it
as though it happened,

Your eyes
seeking mine,
your lips
like fragrant wine,

Tongue exploring,
I unravelled
unravelled…

Transported
through space
and time…

Rhiannon Owens

Face of Stone

His wife pleads with him not to go
to Devil's Rock
it is dangerous up there,
imploring eyes in bruised face
small hands clasped to her bosom.
'Still thy tongue wench'
he pushes her roughly to the ground
jumping into the saddle
and she flinches fearfully,
awaiting the hard slice and sting of the whip
that must surely come,

but he is gone,
she weeps and wails
tugging at her petticoats.

Devil's Rock is actually a cluster of rocks
high-walled, craggy and dense,
there is a cavernous mouth hewn into the cliffs
beside them
where they say a demon guards his gold
and wealth of jewels.
As he grows closer to the looming solidity of stone
the horse begins to buck and rear
whinnying and neighing agitatedly
eyes rolling in fear.
'Forward you stupid beast!'
he kicks at the sleek, muscled flanks
and the horse throws him to the ground,
gallops away, hooves thundering
on hard, unyielding earth.

He has cut his head but will not be deterred,
the mouth of the cave looms ahead
yawning, swallowing the light,
yet as he peers inside he sees something flickering
among the dripping moisture of the stalagmites
and stalactites,
lanterns perhaps...
or the glittering of gold and rubies?
He rubs his greedy hands together.

He is about to step inside when he hears something
a voice - a woman's breathy voice
and he turns to listen
steps away
his quest forgotten.

Yes! There etched into the surface of the rock
a woman's face, exquisite in its detail
exquisite in her beauty.
Intoxicated by the bump to the head
intoxicated by the serene carved face
he approaches her and brushes quivering fingers against her grainy
cheek.
'Speak to me' he murmurs, lovingly tracing
the dusty contours of her features
but she refuses to speak.

'My Love, My Love' he groans
pressing against the rough planes and jagged edges
thrusting against her.
She remains impassive, as unmoved
and unyielding
as that ground had been
'neath the fleeing horse's hooves.

He howls aloud trying to embrace
his heart's desire
with all the agony of a spurned suitor,
shredding his skin, fingers and knuckles
scraping scrabbling
fingernails snap
lips and tongue bloody and torn,
from his attempts to prise
just one warm, sweet kiss
from those cold, perfect lips.

For hours he beseeches her
days, weeks
to no avail, he is exhausted
fingers now worn down to
nothing more than bloody stumps.

There is laughter from within the cave's stagnant belly
cruel and mocking
a demon's high, erratic cackle,
and in a final act of desperation
he dashes his brain out
against the unforgiving cliffside.

Instead of the woman
it is the macabre face of the Devil
that leers down with malicious glee
at his broken, emaciated body
blood draining into, pooling against
cold, grey rock.

Rhiannon Owens

Little Star

There's a very small star
Up in the sky,
It's starting to twinkle
It's catching my eye,

Lying on my bed
Through my window I see,
It twinkles some more
Now it's winking at me,

Am I only dreaming
Would it be a step too far,
To shoot from a cannon
And fly up to that star?

Ashley O'Keefe

Leap of Faith

Here I crouch on bended knee
I'm not getting up until he agrees
to marry me
I'm staying like this 'til he sees
I'm asking him nicely
I even said please
do me the honour.

It's a leap year you see
a day for us women to propose
it's good to take the bull by the horns
at times I suppose
but my knees are aching now
I'd like to repose.

I proffer the ring
the confidence on my face
is belied by the erratic beating
of my heart
as it starts to race.

I can envision it already
our wedding day
me radiant in white
guests happy and gay
us swept up in love's dizzying heights.

I've planned it already
I'm organised
super prepared…
Okay, so I've never met him before
but I wish he'd stop looking so scared!

Rhiannon Owens

Written in the Stars (Etched on my Heart)

Secrets and wishes
thoughts of sweet kisses
all that I want to be mine,
eyes bathed in starlight
moments bathed in pure delight,
all those precious things a heart craves,

Look a little closer...
Will you see them?
The words etched here,
will you read them?
Will you understand them
if I hold you near?

Rhiannon Owens

The Dream that Never Was

I dream of
our first kiss
that never was,
and the first time
we never made love.

Of touching your heart
that stands aloof,
unreachable...

Two hearts beating,
one stripped bare

Of being held
and our pleasures untold,
your hands
your tongue,
my dreams unfold,

Shush now,
not a word
desires that should not
that cannot be,
shouldn't be voiced

Can you keep a secret?
Hush my lips with a kiss

I dream...

I dream of passion
and being filled
with you,
in an inferno of bliss.

Rhiannon Owens

FOLKLORE & FAIRYTALES:

Heart's Desire

Once upon a dream
is where I'll stay, your cold lips
can't tempt me away

He Dances With The Devil

🎻 🎻 🎻 🎻 😺 😺 😺 😺 🎻 🎻

At the stroke of midnight
on what'll be my wedding day
to the finest lady in the land
countin' down the hours,
'til we can be joined, hand in hand.
I look out the window
and I sees the old barn lighted up,
it's lit up all yeller
an' I goes out to see
I'm the darndest foolhardy feller.
See that barn stands empty
we don't use it no more
if we got outlaws hidin' out there
I'm sure gonna be mighty sore…

Where'd he come from
that crazed-lookin' ol' man
with the sparse, white puffs of hair
cackling heehehee, in the darkest corner
of my barn?
Like a sinister marionette,
jerking in a rickety rocking chair
'Hee-heeehee' he goes, his mouth stretches wide,
with one stinking, brown tooth
poking from the rotting inside.
He fixes me with a rheumy, yellow-eyed stare
spits a fat wad of chewing tobacco
on the sawdust floor:

'Come on Boy! It's time to ride!
You're going nowhere nohow
no damn place you can hide!'

I look down at my hands
I'm gripping the finest fiddle
that I ever saw
though I could swear to God
I ain't never seen it before.

Well, now ain't it the strangest
a band strikes up playin'
an' I tuck that fiddle under my chin
like I'd done played it before,
all ready to begin
I brandish the ol' horsehair
and on them strings I saw,
I can't believe it
I really can play
and there's folks all around me
startin' to sway.

Dance dance they chant at me
an' I'm playin', an' I'm dancin'
like my body don't belong to me,
I'm dancin' hard an breakin' a sweat
but somehow it seems
I just can't stop!

Dance dance dance…

Couples twirl as hens peck round their feet
heavy boots stampin' a beat on the floor.
Gals decked out in their best straw bonnets
liftin' swirly, gingham skirts
to show off frilly petticoats,
linkin' arms with men in plaid shirts
who're hopin' to see more…

but me, I can't stop playin'
I'm feelin' desperate now!

Bobbin' and weavin' round stacks of hay
watched by fat grey rats
with baleful eyes...
big fat rats; bigger'n cats,
Hell, bigger than coyotes!
Glaring, pink-eyed as I continue to play.
I need to stop, my fingers are all blistered and raw,
there's smoke comin' from my damn fingertips:
I can't play no more!

... but maybe...

if I can keep playing through the first light of dawn
if I can just do it 'til the blessed, sweet morn'
there's just three more hours to go...

Do not forsake me oh my darlin'...

She was all dressed up for her wedding day
when she found him in his empty barn,
laid out in a dirty, old scattering of hay.
Lying face down, and so terribly still
she hardly dared turn him around
and she screamed and backed away,
at what she found.

His eyes open wide, his face all charred
his hands and fingers mangled and bleeding
white bone glinting,
he was permanently scarred.

Some of the farmhands took him to his bed

he breathed still but never moved
just kept on staring fixedly
straight ahead.
Her fine man, her sweetheart
her intended;
in a catatonic state.
No flicker of life, nor love for her
and, save the burns,
no physical signs of illness
no fever or accelerated heart rate.

I can't understand why life goes on the way it does?
Must I just sit here and watch him die?
Oh, do not forsake me, oh my darling!
Look how these tired eyes of mine cry!

He's stuck in that ol' Barn Dance
and it's a dance come straight from Hell
and the folks just keep on dancing
as the flames rise higher and swell,
and he plays on that fiddle
and the band they are a-singing,
the folks are all coupled up
they are swinging, they are flinging…
Dance dance dance
an' that violin is smoking!
Play play play
on the black fumes he is choking!
Dance dance dance
Play play play
and the men's pricks are a-poking,
and the women's eyes are red
and their twisted legs are spread,
and out of their cavernous, gaping sex
vicious teeth plunge into

the shiny, purple-veined heads.

This is a shin-dig that never ends
can't you hear the whistle of the Death Train?
The neighing and stomping of horses
that aren't really there
and the Devil's music,
and the shrieks and agonising screams
of the insane.
The ceiling is gone but there are no stars to be seen
twinkling up above in place of the old wooden beams,
instead there is only a blood red sky
with a pulsing blackhole
seeping pus from a giant, disease-ridden eye.

Everyone in here, they

Burn
Burn
Burn…

The train it is a-comin'
and they all walk the line.
Look! Now it's your turn…

The Ghost Riders round up anyone, who tries to stray,
once that fiddle builds up steam, you can't get away.
All you can hear is this terrible soundtrack.
Don't you know it's The End of the World?
Skin melts from bones
like sick, yellowed wax,
innards spill in gelatinous blood and tissue swirls.

Dance dance dance…

round that Ring of Fire,
watching all the time as those flames
keep on creeping higher.
Yeeeeee-haawww, there's no end to this dance tonight
the Devil's debauched carnival
for his insatiable, sadistic appetite.
Pitchforks stab at you
force you closer, to that ring of fire
the festering bowels of Hell
the chthonic underbelly,
a soul-sucking bottomless well.

See the coven huddled at the side
around a corpse they're stripping bare,
no fear from them
of the devil and his underground lair.
These harridans are the source
of an ancient, dark dark power,
and all who meet their sightless eyes
sink to their knees and cower.
A gnarled daemon with xanthic eyes
suckles on a hag's black, withered dug
the greenish, milky bile spills down his deformed face
his stiffened cock a filthy nub
that leaves a silvery snail trail,
all viscous; slimy like a slug.
The crones gorge on the rotted carcass
smacking dried out, scaly lips,
one masturbates with a finger bone
rocking her emaciated, skeletal hips.

In the bed, his burns are spreading more and more
as the days go by,
and no doctor or physician across the land,
is able to say why.

I never made it out of that barn
I never did see the dawn
I never could drop that fiddle
Never saw the light of the morn'...

I danced, danced, danced
and my darlin' I did play,
please do not forsake me
on this our wedding day...

The wedding would have been long ago,
his body deteriorates in that bed
the burns eating, consuming his flesh,
a weaker woman than her
by now, surely would have fled,
but though she knows he's lost to her
she chooses to stay instead,
in her tattered wedding finery
weeping by his side
every now and then she raises her head
this tragic, tormented bride.
She fancies she can hear a fiddle playing
over in that empty barn
and though the music is enticing
she knows he wants her beside him,
wants to keep his wife safe from harm,
he never will forsake her
because he loves her dear,
and so he will never condemn her
to the Devil's base and bestial charm.

Rhiannon Owens
**(Inspired by and a tribute to 'High Noon' plus artists such as Johnny Cash,
Skeeter Davis and the Charlie Daniels band).**

Treasure

There once was a shoemaker
Who through no fault of his own,
Became very poor
His last pair of shoes to be sewn,

That evening he cut
His final pieces of leather,
On his worktable, he left them
Then to bed; dreaming of treasure,

Falling asleep
Lying on his bed,
Asking God for help
Saying prayers in his head,

Morning soon came
Sitting down to his work,
Two shoes standing; finished
Was it time for him to lurk?

Taking the shoes
He looked more closely,
So neat, so perfect
He was astounded mostly,

The shop doorbell rang
A customer did seize,
Paying double the price
For these fine shoes that did please,

The shoemaker now
With more money for the leather,
Could make two pairs of shoes
Suddenly seeing his treasure,

The same again
The very next day,
Two pairs of shoes
Like masterpieces, they lay,

With no shortage of customers
This went on and on,
The shoemaker became rich
With customers singing his song,

Then one evening before Christmas
He cut out the leather,
And said to his wife
"Let's see who's giving us this treasure",

His wife liked the idea
They would now know for certain,
Who was helping them out
So they hid behind a curtain,

And as the clock struck midnight
Two little elves came out,
And got straight to work
But for clothes, they were without,

The shoemaker and his wife
Looked at each other,
A tear in their eye
These elves needed some cover,

These little naked men
Had now made them rich,
So to show they were grateful
New clothes the wife would stitch,

And her husband would make

Two small pairs of shoes,
The shoemaker and his wife
Now paying their dues,

One night they lay
Their gifts on the worktable,
Instead of the leather
New clothes and shoes to enable,

At midnight the elves appeared
Ready to do their work,
But were puzzled by the clothes
And the job they now shirk,

Delighted, they dressed
And put the fine clothes on,
They danced and they sang
Yes, they sang this sweet song,

"Now we are boys so fine to see,
Why should we longer cobblers be?"

They danced and skipped
And leapt in the air,
They danced out the door
Without a care,

The elves never returned
Never again to see,
But business now prospered
And the old couple lived happily...

... Ever after.

Ashley O'Keefe
(Inspired by 'The Elves and the Shoemaker' story which my Grandmother used to read to me as a child – A treasured memory)

The Witches Brew

Boil the water in the pot,
Fetch a toddler from its cot,
Drop it in the cauldron there,
With intestines from grizzly bear,
Sprinkle with blood, and mix for an hour,
To give a very special power,
Add frogs and snails,
Quails,
And rat's tails,
Season with lungs,
And Demon's tongues,
Spider's legs, and soldier's foot,
A couple of ants, and some soot,
Viper's venom, bulldog's bite,
Just a touch of pepper,
To make it right,
Black rose's thorn,
A Devil's horn,
A murder victim's scream,
Drinking this potion will be a nightmare,
But it'll work like a dream…
A clash of thunder, a lightning streak,
A bit of kidney, a dead man's shriek,
Black magic from a witch's hat,
A pumpkin, and a big, black bat,
Add some fireworks to make pops and bangs,
A piece of heart, and vampire's fangs,
Bits of spine, and limbs, and bones,
And a box of moans and groans,
Fragments from a turtle's shell,
And all the darkest powers of Hell,
Now it smokes, and fizzes, and steams,
Add some stars, and now it gleams,

Now you hear a sizzle and a boom,
Stir well with witch's broom,
Rock goes in from the moon,
And a corpse, from its tomb,
Now the brew is ready to drink,
Evil, deadly, black as ink,
Get a cup,
Drink it up.

Rhiannon Owens

Guardian Angels

We all have guardian angels
Watching over us,
Guiding and protecting
Through life's pathways, dawn till dusk,

They come in all shapes and forms
They do not all have angel wings,
One day they walk into our lives
Let us see what tomorrow brings.

Ashley O'Keefe

A Little Leprechaun

I saw a little leprechaun,
Surrounded by his money,
The only food he had with him,
Were little jars of honey.
I thought if I could get his gold,
It'd be my lucky day,
But then he turned and saw me,
And he upped and ran away.
It started to rain upon my head,
And I began to catch a cold,
But I couldn't let the leprechaun escape,
With all those pots of gold.
But when I turned the corner,
My leprechaun had fled,
So away I turned, homeward bound,
To rest my weary head!

Rhiannon Owens

The Three Billy Goats Gruff

Once upon a time…
The Three Billy Goats Gruff,
Went up to the hillside
To fatten and to stuff,

On the way to the hill
Over a cascading stream,
There's a small wooden bridge
Beneath, an ugly troll in a dream,

With eyes like saucers
A long nose like a spout,
He's big and he's ugly
Chews and spits your bones out…

First across went the youngest Billy Goat Gruff…
"Trip, trap, trip, trap!"

"Who's that tripping and trapping?"
Roared the troll in a huff,

A small voice cries
"It's only I, tiny Billy Goat Gruff"

"Well I'm coming to eat you
You'll be gone in a puff"

"Oh no! I'm too little"
My brother's bigger than me,
Wait 'til he crosses
He's behind me, you'll see…

Next across went the middle Billy Goat Gruff…

"Trip, trap, trip, trap!"

"Who's that tripping and trapping?"
Roared the troll in a huff,

A low voice speaks
"It's only I, middle Billy Goat Gruff"

"Well I'm coming to eat you
You'll be gone in a puff"

"Oh no! I'm too small"
My brother's bigger than me,
Wait 'til he crosses
He's behind me, you'll see…

Last to go across went the big Billy Goat Gruff…
"Clip, clap, clip, clap!"

"Who's that clipping and clapping?"
Roared the troll in a huff,

A big voice booms
"It's I, big Billy Goat Gruff"

"Well I'm coming to eat you
You'll be gone in a puff"

"Oh no! You won't"
I've got sharp horns you see,
Your eyes, I'll poke out
And crush your body internally,

Then charging at the troll
He poked out his eyes,

Crushed his bones and tossed him
Over the bridge, then he sighs,

Trotting up to the hillside
Joining his brothers,
Where they eat all they can
Upon those green folding covers.

Ashley O'Keefe

Breathtaking

Each night I'd lie in bed
frightened, because I'd heard tell
of the stealer of breath.
She knows no boundaries
cares not of your sex,
her mouth fastens over yours
taking your final breath.

I've often sat up in the dark
sure that she'll come
but always thought I would fight
never succumb.

Here she is.
Ice blue eyes gaze into mine
a flinty, sharpened, penetrative gaze,
silver glinting in her ice-white hair
bloodless blue lips
still inviting,
still plump
and ripe.

They warned me she'd suck
the very breath from my body,
destroy me with her kiss of death
sucking me dry

but as her lips meet mine
they are gentle
but cold
oh god, so very cold
but so tantalisingly gentle too.

It's like being immersed
in the most frigid of places,
doused head-to-toe in a freezing sea of ice.
A kiss that takes your breath away,
she's breathtaking
has literally stolen my breath away.

My breathing has stopped
my heart frozen over
so cold that it bites
a cold so biting
so painful,
that it actually scalds.

Scalding passions
unexpected
unleashed
untamed.

'I can't do it to you'
her hoarse whisper hangs in the air,
she just yearns for love
companionship.

Before the icy paralysis sets in
our hands reach and grip,
fingers interlocking
and
she looks at me
and
I gaze back at her.

Lips pressed together
tongues probe
we breathe each other in,
taking yet sharing.

Her tears run down
her beautiful face
onto mine;
no droplets of ice
her tears are ripe,
they are hopeful and warm.
My tears are hot.
We melt into each other's arms.

Rhiannon Owens

More Than Just Ashes

Worth more than just ashes
More than sacrifice,
Her compassion and kindness
So humble, so nice,
Beauty within
Beauty inside and out,
So lonely, so abused
So given the runabout,
Worthy of happiness
With a warm-hearted man,
Self-worth and respect
With her Prince while she can.

Ashley O'Keefe

Beauty

So hideous, so ugly
how can she ever see,
the beating heart
so full of love,
behind the horror that is me?

"I love his face
his kind kind eyes,
how can he love me
at all...
so generic, so dull
I neither roar
nor fly...
how could I ever expect

to make him love,
or to hear him sigh?"

*She clutches at my
fearsome paw,
I try to push her away
frighten with my ferocious roar,
but she only clasps
more firmly...
she seems to want me even more...*

"I have nothing to offer
so paltry
so poor,
how could I even dare
to believe
that I could make
his big heart soar?"

***Little hand
twined with shiny claws,
no beast exists
within beauty,
they are love
truly, pure...
forever
evermore!***

Rhiannon Owens

The Gift Inside

"Mirror, Mirror,
Speak to me,
Cast your eyes
Tell me all you see,

"You are…",

The poisoned apple
The bitter pill,

Putrescent and pungent
A decaying chill,

Lacking in warmth
And sunshine of the soul,

All wrapping paper
The gift inside; stole,

"Mirror, Mirror,
Tell me all you see,
Cast your eyes
This cannot be",

The fair-hearted one
Truly outshines,
In the deepest forests
Near dwarven mines…

Ashley O'Keefe

Poison (Snow White)

She had hair as black as Schwartzkopf hair dye
would allow,
skin as white as a year spent in lockdown
without so much as an outing to Rhyl,
and lips as red as the red red wine she was slugging
chased down with a couple of pills...

Snow White had left the castle,
her stepmother was a right old witch
so she'd shacked up with seven dwarfs,
who always worked double-shifts,

but her stepmother turned up
disguised as an old woman,
tempting her with various wares,
that were all laced with poison.

Lace for her corset...
Corset??? She laughed,
I'm not bloody kinky
these bad girls of mine are fine enough
in this wonder bra as modelled by Holly Willoughby,
thank you very much!

Then a comb...
A comb???
I just forked out for this trendy bob,
for God's sake,
I don't need to comb this sleek hairdo
just run my fingers through it
and give it a shake!

The final temptation an apple,

all juicy and rosy and ripe…
An apple???
Oh Luv, you must be joking,
I'm on the Atkins diet!
She exhales nicotine-tinged breath
into the old woman's face
as she's busily chain-smoking.

The silly old bat finally gave up,
and Snow White set traps to get rid of the birds, the rabbits,
all the bloody vermin,
everything was sweet...
but then the dwarfs were made redundant…
suddenly everything became more Grimm…

Snow White had already murdered a Huntsman
smashing his head in with his own axe,
she'd taken his heart as a trophy,
her first kill but not her last...

She trapped the dwarfs in a glass coffin,
watched them try to break free,
Dopey all oblivious,
Happy at last scuppered,
and finally a legit reason for Grumpy.

Hey boys, she says with a snigger,
don't be Bashful,
should I call for a Doc...
Hey boys,
this is nothing to be Sneezed at...
she slaps her thigh
roars in laughter,
they grow Sleepy,
she grows bored and so

swigging from her can of special brew,
she leaves all seven of them to rot.

The Queen stomps around the castle,
all newly botoxed, full of fillers and the like,
she shoots a gaze across the room,
fixes her reflection with a cold hard stare

Mirror Mirror on the wall
who is the fairest of them all?

The mirror sighs,
its breath misting the opaque glass,
Oh, Queen when will you realise,
I'm just a mirror, I don't bloody care!

Rhiannon Owens

Lost in the Woods

Abandoned, neglected,
Emotionally abused,
A Brother and Sister
Lost in the woods and confused,

They go to the Sweet House
Of a psychopathic witch,
Using her sweetness
To mask evil, the bitch!

A story of horror
Parental neglect,
Emotional indifference
Leading children to inflect,

Robbing them of love
And a way to find home,
Without emotional safety
Or security, they roam.

Ashley O'Keefe

The Dragon and the Silly Knight

Upon the hill, the Dragon sat,
Breathing his orange fire,
The smoke crept down to the village,
And drove the people quite haywire.

"We must get rid of the Dragon,"
Said the people in despair,
So they called upon the Silly Knight,
To give the Dragon a scare.

The Silly Knight ran up the hill,
And soon he reached the top,
But when he reached the Dragon's cave,
He felt he had to stop.

"Alright Dragon, you've had your chips,
I'll turn you into mince,
And when I get back to the village,
I'll be treated like a Prince!"

The Dragon shook his mighty head,
And said "No, I don't think so,
Please excuse my impoliteness,
But you'll simply have to go."

The Silly Knight was defeated,
So he went back to his home,
The villagers now ignore him,
While the Dragon's left to roam!

Rhiannon Owens

Beauty Reclining

A silent sleeping kingdom
where not a creature stirs

A Princess of the Dawn
lies silently inert
from a sleeping curse

The phallic prick
of a phallic spindle
left her in this passive recline

but a Handsome Prince is on his way
"I shall make her mine!"

With phallic arrogance
he chops down phallic thorns
with an over-sized phallic sword

on and on he battles
even as he yawns

… But nobody asked this Sleeping Beauty
what it is SHE wants…

Since childhood she's been locked away:

Locked in Castle
Locked in Sleep
Locked in 'Love'...

Now she's broken free
in her private Dreamworld
slumbering forever
slumbering deep

in a place where she can always be beautiful
one day she might choose to wake again...

but till then the whole kingdom shall sleep!

Rhiannon Owens

Fairytale Ending

Standing proud
Standing strong,
As if conjured from
A fairytale song,

Walls for protection
Towers; far to see,
A place to shelter
Its community,

Through the courtyards
Through the great halls,
Echoes of joy
Sounds of applause,

Singing, dancing

Sweet music plays,
On one of those royal
Fairytale wedding days.

Ashley O'Keefe
(Inspired by all those films and stories I used to watch and read with my girls when they were small)

Thumbelina

She would dance
and she would sing,
and curl into the flowers
a tiny little thing,
friend to birds
but not rain showers,

Miniscule petalled skirt
sewn from spider's web,
delicate as the blooms
that she calls her bed,

Then all the birds migrate,
her friends,
the nest she saw as home
but a tiny boy bows
"I'm Tom Thumb.."
perhaps she need not be alone...

Rhiannon Owens
(I realise Thumbelina and Tom Thumb never met but they could have been great together)

Birdsong

Once upon a time there was a woman who loved too much, and she was vulnerable and stupid, her head in the clouds, so she was always used but never loved.

Then, one day she found a beautiful man. The two of them had been previously stung, and they forged a life of love together. The two of them, so glad to have been found. Yet, the years went by and the love seemed to stall...

it wasn't the way they had wanted at all!

... and the woman's heart ached and went into free-fall. She opened her eyes, her heart was all aflutter, but it was all wrong, with feelings she could never utter.

So, each night she walked barefoot through the forest, oblivious to snow, wind and rain. Clutching her heart and feeling so lonely, immune to the numbness of frostbitten pain.

Walking and walking, clearing her mind. Crying salt tears that never did stop. Walking and walking. Crying, crying...

One day she could walk no further, and she opened her reddened eyes wide. For, a man waited still for her at home, and she had promised to always be his bride.

Through thick and through thin. A love shared...

and she'd walked and she'd walked as those tears spilled. Walked on and on, as they fell all around, walked further still... they poured down all the more, and now she blinks and walks to her door, leaving those tears behind... but if she turned she would see, just what those loving tears had become. For each pure salt tear, every sparkling diamond of woe, a teeny-tiny, colourful bird is born...

because beauty is born from both joy and sorrow, and all love exists in beautiful thoughts...

and each bird flutters and hops, and takes to the sky, singing the sweetest of songs that will never die...

Rhiannon Owens

Echo & Narcissus

Sweet Nymph of loose lips
is silenced,
just an echo of a voice that had rang out long and clear,
she falls in love with a beautiful youth,
longing to touch him, to hold him near,

He hears her footsteps and calls out
'Who is there?'
in vain she tries to make her voice heard,
but *'There... there... there...'*
echoed back at him,
is all the golden youth can hear,

Her passion for him grows ever stronger
and she runs to him,
ready to be folded into his sweet embrace,
but he draws away, spurns her
cruel face twisted with distaste,

'Hands off! May I die before you enjoy my body!'
and the Nymph simply whispers
'Enjoy my body...'
with bitter tears blinding her eyes
as she flees,

In humiliation and shame she weeps
but her ardour grows evermore,
and the vain youth lies by the river,
catches a glimpse of his own reflection
and sees the only face he could ever adore,

Pleading his words of love,
but the face he sees only mimics him,
and he grows anguished
'Why do you mock me?'
and the words bounce off the trees,
'Me... Me... Me...'
and he pines away from this love unrequited,
youthful vanity was his sin,

... and the sweet Nymph is thrown into despair,
from seeing the beautiful youth wasted away,
and she pines and she fades,
and her heart turns to stone...

but her sweet voice whispers on,
lingers,
it haunts us,
an echo that can still be heard to this day.

Rhiannon Owens
(Inspired by the story of Echo and Narcissus in Greek Mythology)

HORROR & THE SUPERNATURAL:

Shivers down your spine…
Flesh mottled with goose pimples…
Foul breath lifts your hair…

Pumpkin Surprise

Cut off the tops
Scoop out the insides,
Give them to Mother
For pumpkin pie surprise,

Wielding the blade
Cut out the face,
With the scariest scowl
Evil eyes in place,

With candles inside
Make them ignite,
Then all is ready
For this howling fright night.

Ashley O'Keefe

Pumpkin

The pumpkin seemed to stare at me
from out of the pitch-black night,
I was tipsy from the Halloween party,
hadn't expected it to be there
so it gave me a bit of a fright,
smiling at me in sinister fashion
leering, with its maw of jagged delight,
those gaping triangles illuminating its hollow innards,
the flickering flame giving the unsettling illusion of sight.

Feeling foolish, I wished that the candle would die,
a spiteful fantasy to crush up the orange vegetable

mash it into pulp for a pumpkin pie!
I gave it a vicious kick
and the light was instantly snuffed out,
I laughed at my sad victory when I should have been wondering
why,
in my mind there should have been doubts…

Why was the pumpkin on my doorstep?

Who had lit a candle and left the lantern lying about?

I'd stupidly cut off my only source of light,
I clumsily fumbled for my keys
as a figure lunged from the shadows,
hands crushing my throat,
squeezing tight,
my feet kicked at the dirt
as I was dragged into the night,
there'd been no time for me to scream
or shout…

Colours and shapes burst behind my eyelids,
blooming, flaring so devastatingly bright,
and the pumpkin is probably still sinisterly smiling
as just like that candle,
I am entirely snuffed out.

Rhiannon Owens

Night

Night...

The curtain closing
The dying of the light,

Darkness comes...

Erasing sight,

Open eyes see nothing
Closed eyes see all night,

Until dawn's song approaches...

When black fades back to light.

Ashley O'Keefe

Crazy Horses Around the Outside

Making a bid for freedom
sick of the childish sound
sick of the dizzying whirling
I'm vacating this merry-go-round.

The pissed-up blokes on stag do's
the kids with the leaking nappies
the fat-arsed mid-life crisis folk
I'm off cantering, I want to be happy!

No longer will I sit there
a zombie to your tune

we're gathering a carousel rebel army
there'll be none of us to ride very soon.

I want to gallop along the beach
feel the wind in my plastic-coated mane
I want to be free like Black Beauty
away from this 'Bobby Horse' pain!

Rhiannon Owens

What Lies Within

The sky lights up
A deafening roar,
The lashing rain
The heavy downpour,

A house lights up
Upon the hill,
A stormy night
The ghastly chill,

Haunting, scary
What lies within,
Soaked right through
To bone and skin,

Through the gates
With heavy groan,
Ring the bell
There's an alarming moan,

A howling wind
The darkest night,

The door creaks open
The terror... the bite.

Ashley O'Keefe

Demon Born

Something within me has started to decay,
and with the rot comes darkness,
I take your children and break your hearts.
Then I break your bones
drag you down into the ground,
force you to confess
feasting on your sick souls,
devouring you, hearing your helpless moans,
till there is nothing left
save a blood and entrail mess.
Your body burns,
all melting skin
in
my blazing inferno of sweet smelted sin.

Rhiannon Owens

Blood Moon

The dark of night is beginning to draw in
on this All Hallows Eve,
full moon casting ghostly luminescence
across the gloom,
strange, there was no full moon forecast tonight
yet here it is piercing the forbidding shadows,
a tiny bit of light retrieved.
Something is not right,
the animals sense an electricity in the air,
caterwauling cats scrambling for cat-flaps
wanting sanctuary
and dogs howling, eyes like saucers
with a terrified, glassy stare,
the cats are like aged punk-rockers
arched spines that stiffly bristle with erect fur.
Indoors, canaries circle crazily around their cages
in a fluttering frenzy of fear,
round, round, round…
hamsters in their plastic balls
are running, running, running
fruitlessly,
desperate to get away, to be anywhere but here!
Something has settled over this small town
like an insidious blanket,
dirty, moth-eaten and stinking
and all at once, the adults doing adult things
stop, turn, listen…
and as one drift out of their homes
dropping glasses and plates, disregarding meals,
children are forgotten about, lovers spurned,
their synapses burn,
eyes drawn to the moon, the blood-red moon
and they follow it…

In the woods, a group of teens,
the greatest cliche of Halloween!
A sexy ladybird, a slinky cat, a slutty nurse
and a handful of horror film killers.
Kreuger has been stuck at second base
with the kitty-cat for a while,
tonight he's geared up for the home run,
he's heard that the nurse goes the extra mile
and should've opted for her
because Florence Nightingale she ain't
and it's a challenge getting this pussy *sniggers* to purr.
Packs of beer abound to aid them all on their mission,
get them loosened up, get them laid,
here in the woods, far from prying eyes
and parental supervision.

They are not the only ones in the woods,
here come the little adventurers
a group of kids,
the too old for toys, too young for boys
girly brigade,
snuck out of the house too mature for silly sleepovers,
too grown-up for Halloween costumes,
dressing up is for babies,
venturing into the night to prove how adult they are,
how they aren't *voices quiver, chins wobble, lips tremble*
afraid…

The adults are gathering in the woods
gazing up and chanting at the moon,
their clothes have all been discarded
skin of all shades and tones illumed.
A figure in tattered robes stands before them
arms raised up high,
he has the head of a wolf

and he bays at his new pack
as they remain hypnotised,
naked beneath the ominous skies.
The chanting increases in volume,
then there's a crescendo of pain
and metamorphosis,
they are changing
features elongating here, blunted there
their minds snapped and bent,
they are becoming insane...

The troop of girls are following the torchlight
when they hear the agonised inhuman sounds,
'What's that?" quavers Emily
and the girls all pull closer,
save for Elsie who runs away
deeper into the merciless woods,
stumbling, weeping,
then a high-pitched scream, cut short
and she is gone, never again to be found.

'The fuck was that?' Kreuger says
his beer goggles squinting blearily,
primed more for tits than trees.
The ladybird with the nice arse says
'I heard a scream... did you?'
and he gives her bum a clumsy squeeze
to put her at ease.
The bargain-bucket Michael Myers says
'I think we should get out of these woods'
as there is rustling in the branches
and shadows are skittering about the undergrowth.
Leave? It's sweet that they honestly believe they could!

Emily is still following the light

as it bobs just ahead of her.
Karen has the torch,
and though it's only a sad pinprick really
she's determined not to let it out of her sight,
she won't be left behind
to whatever fate befell Elsie,
Elsie who was always so nice, so kind
but Emily can't even cry for her friend
she's just feeling so numb,
she prays Karen knows which way to go
she needs this night to end, she is done.
One foot in front of another
and then she's sinking,
into the soft marshy ground,
'Just like that' she thinks miserably,
she fell for the oldest trick in the book
and now just like Elsie, she'll never be found.
'I wonder where Karen really is?' is her last thought
as she is sucked down,
and she does not utter a sound
as the foul-smelling bog water fills her mouth,
her nose,
not one sound uttered as she drowns.

Karen is following the light,
Emily must have the torch.
Karen is brave and bold - the leader of their group,
the rebel, the one who will not do as she's told!
She strides along with confidence
but then her foot becomes caught,
tangled up in something sticky
but as she kicks at it she becomes more enmeshed,
the more she panics, the worse it gets,
she fights and the tacky strands become impossibly taut.
A web… the thought flickers through her head

as a toxic paralysis immobilises her,
a mummified delicacy all gift-wrapped
ready for when the spider alights from its bed
ready to break the fast,
staring up from her suffocating trap
she sees the eight-legged behemoth,
all bristled and ghastly and incisored,
but sleeping peacefully.
When those eight eyes stare into her own,
and she sees her own pale reflection in them,
she'll know the final die has been cast,
but... she fixes her fading eyes on the beast again,
why hadn't it been alerted to the web's vibrations?
Could it be? Yes... somehow the beast has been skewered,
run through by a branch,
her sluggish heart almost bursts with elation.
The spider is dead and though she's stuck
there's light at the end of the tunnel,
Karen smiles into the darkness,
unable to believe her luck.
Then,
Screeeeeeeeee
shatters her eardrums, a shriek reverberating in her brain,
the darkness seems to have become even deeper,
a mutated, gargantuan bird of prey up above,
a butcher bird, with deadly beak
gleaming like the scythe of the Grim Reaper.
Karen is carried through the air
by the razor grip of this screaming banshee
and her bravado disappears and she quails,
then she's falling, the hunter drops her onto a splintered bough,
her throat and chest speared
easy as unrefrigerated butter,
as she is savagely impaled.

Somehow, the piss-poor fire that the lad in the hockey mask had built
has gone haywire, a blazing inferno,
flames raging across the dead leaves and branches,
the teenagers are able to take in the show.
Nudity all around them,
looking like people but their movements are more agile,
they are feral, bestial
and their faces all wrong.
One is vulpine, full of foxy wiles,
cunning, slanted eyes.
Another, all flattened snout,
here, a small-breasted woman with tapered face
and a reptilian tongue flickering,
forked and long
with venom dripping from full, fat sacs.
The youths try to run
but they should have been watching their backs.
Flesh tears and bones crack
as the predatory beings bring them down,
feasting, gorging, swallowing steaming entrails,
the once upstanding folk of a small, upstanding town.

Ali is not following the light,
she knows Elsie was carrying the torch, and
she's watched loads of horror films and things
with her older sister,
she's not stupid, she knows what that light means,
the death that the ghost-lights will bring.
Too smart to be guided by a Wil-o'-the-Wisp,
she has spotted a well-worn path,
too clever to be lured into an early grave
or end up right in the midst of some grisly bloodbath.
Ali follows the path as it winds and swerves
and eventually it pays off, the open road is ahead,

when suddenly, a plaintive cry is carried on the faint breeze,
like the mewling of an infant... alone in this forest?
Ali hesitates - she can't let a baby die of exposure,
she changes direction instead,
steps off the path and into the trees.
In a small clearing, a baby lies, half-swaddled,
little fists beating the air, face mottled purple
as it cries and it cries,
Ali walks across and gathers the poor little thing into her arms,
cradling it as she does her baby brother
but when she looks into its face again,
she goes rigid with alarm.
The eyes have no pupils, they are twin xanthic
orbs,
and the face is beginning to scale over,
there are bony ridges at the forehead,
this is no sweet babe for a mother to adore.
Clawed hands swipe across her cheek,
shredding skin
and Ali cries out and casts the monstrosity away,
she runs like the hounds of hell are at her heels
hoping to get back on that open road,
hoping she's going back the right way.
The wails of a baby all around, ringing in her ears
at every twist and turn the crying is louder
more persistent,
it should be in the distance, not sounding so near...
No no,
Ali is weeping
as she finds herself back in that clearing,
and the deformed creature springs,
teeth sink into her jugular...
'A Tiyanak' is her last thought,
an old movie playing in her head, reeling
while the monster keeps on feeding.

There are fissures in the earth,
the feral townsfolk all tumble like ragdolls,
falling pell-mell
and lying prone on the floor,
their features are beginning to soften again
but all their vitality, their essence
is being siphoned into the bowels of hell,
until they lie desiccated, just dry husks
neither human nor animal anymore.
The blood-red moon is maliciously grinning
from its VIP seat way up high,
a Jack o' Lantern face leering down, and Jack intones,
'Tonight, everyone will die!'
The grin on his sly face grows wider
like a pregnant belly fit to burst,
stretching until it splits open
spilling out its black-hearted curse
in a downpour of innards and blood,
that seals up all the fissures,
but has not yet quenched the Devil's thirst...
and all through the town the terrible blood-rain falls,
reaching, spreading, a viscous, crimson flood.

When the morning finally arrives
and the winter sun does not rise,
the red waters are lying motionless,
a vista for nobody's eyes.
Not a creature in this town is stirring,
no sign of any people anywhere.
There's the heavy silence of death in the air,
the silence is just hanging there
and it seems to grow and grow
for everyone has disappeared without a trace,
save for the pets that remain in the houses
frozen in an unhallowed permanent tableau

with fixed rictus grimace on petrified face.

Rhiannon Owens

Mind of Echoes

A deafening explosion
A fiery ball,
Of yellow flame
A violent blast, befall,

Billowing outwards
A gush of flame,
Fiery smoke
With debris to maim,

A howling horror
A fearful blow,
A wave of dust
Like fiery snow,

Smoke; choking,
Ringing in the ears,
Eyes blurring
Burning tears,

A mind of echoes
Reverberating around,
Then all falls silent
Dust settles, no sound...

... Suddenly a whimper
Then comes a cry,
The movement of rubble

Who lives, who will die?

Ashley O'Keefe

Shards

The
Stairs
Creaking
In the night
As shadows draw in
So hard to hear in the silence
Is that the sound of heavy feet dragging on carpet?
The door bursts open and my mirror shatters sending a thousand
shards to pierce my heart

Rhiannon Owens

The Candle

Sounds from the attic
And the cellar below,
The banging window
The howling wind and the snow,

The slamming door
It groans and creaks,
And keeps on thumping
On a hinge that squeaks,

The candle blows out
Losing its flame,

In the darkness, the fear
Drives me insane,

Touching and bumping
Walking into things,
I panic in fright
As I hear flapping wings,

Relighting the candle
Igniting the flame,
See the curtains flapping
My pounding heart I must tame,

No longer alone
I'm inside your room,
Glimpse the fiend above you
In the darkened gloom,

The groans, the creaking
Coming from your bed,
Then he turns to me
Eyes blood-shot red,

Glaring, piercing
My voice whispers your name,
The candle blows out
Losing its flame.

Ashley O'Keefe

Sweet Dreams, Sleep Tight

The little girl's eyes are like saucers
in the fading light,
fixed on the life-sized doll,
there'll be no sleep for her tonight.
Its eyes are gleaming glass
that are preternaturally bright,
how can she settle down
when she is at the mercy of its sight?
She starts to cry,
her mum is alerted to her plight
and turns the doll to face the wall,
plants a soft kiss,
"Nothing to fear darling, snuggle up,
sweet dreams, sleep tight."

A spider scurries across the doll's face,
invisible in the dimming light,
chased by an invisible tear,
there'll be no comfort for her tonight.
Her eyes long to close
and dream of a life that is warm and bright,
where little children are cheered,
when, of her, they catch a sight.
Crying soundlessly, wordless
with no one to save her from her plight,
facing the comfortless wall,
wishing the little girl would snuggle up with her,
and softly whisper
"sweet dreams, sleep tight."

Rhiannon Owens

TORTURED PLEASURES:

Torture?

*Feverish desires
a lot of pleasure to be
gained... amongst the pain!*

Spectre of Desire

Alone in my bedroom
then suddenly you are there
fingers undressing me
leaving me bare
and nakedly vulnerable
but visibly aroused

for my awkwardness you have not a care
stroking me with a soft yet persistent touch
fire and ice
I'm feverish
it all becomes too much
I can't, I just can't take any more
then a rush of relief
a surge from deep within my core
rushing from inside
a roaring tide

I look for you
with hopeful eyes
but my room is empty
I'm left with nothing
but slick, sticky thighs
and once again
I'm all alone
anguished now
because
you made me feel whole.

Rhiannon Owens

Only in Dreams

Only in dreams
Making love through the night,
Breathing in rhythm
In our climaxing flight,

Like a ship at sea
During the storm,
We ride those waves
We find our way home,

In our seesaw ride
We play with the rhyme,
Discover new highs
In simultaneous time,

In breathless pleasure
We wash up on the shore,
We smile to the skies
As our bodies crave more.

Suddenly I'm waking
Opening my eyes,
I stare at the ceiling
And miss those sweet sighs.

Ashley O'Keefe

Where I Can Live in My Head

Snail-like, curled inside a shell
Lightly cocooned
Under my duvet
Glowing all flushed and rosy
As I dream of the forbidden
Buried in erotic pleasure
Endless bliss... I think I'll stay in this
Dreamworld, in my head and my bed forever!

Rhiannon Owens
(A 'Slugabed' is a person who stays in bed after the usual/proper time to get up)

Amongst the Dunes

Rising from the waves
A sunny beach of gold,
Resplendent sands stretching out
Along its shores the ocean rolled,

Upon buoyant waves come riding
The flora of a salty sea,
Deeply green left on the beach
Ocean aroma rich algae,

The tall grass amongst the dunes
Whispers softly in the breeze,
Sand grains gust, get in our eyes
And makes us want to sneeze,

Lying here beside you
Away from the beach,

151

Time stands still for no one...
You'll soon be out of reach.

Ashley O'Keefe

Illicit

The heat is rising
Rising as I break into a sweat, perspiring
Perspiring because I'm desiring,
Desiring what only you can provide,
Provide me with this feeling,
Feeling dizzy, I am reeling,
Reeling but you draw me in
Into our delicious sin,
Sin that feels so divine,
Divine because for one moment you're mine,
Mine, rocking with our own rhythm and cadence,
Cadence that only we can sense,
Sense and understand,
Understand, we join hands,
Hands that tingle because we found our own tune to dance to,
To sigh, pulsate, encapsulate,
Encapsulate this wicked sliver of forbidden passion,
Passion forbidden but passion that delights,
Delights that have us shuddering into the greatest heights,
Heights that should never have been reached,
Reached, scaled, peaked and it felt so right.

Rhiannon Owens

Your Fantasy

A dream, a fantasy
Before your eyes,
Slipping smoothly
Between your thighs,

Tenderly kissing
Face and neck,
French kissing
A teasing peck,

Nibbling earlobes
Tongue caressing ear,
Your seductive lips
Sensational rear,

Tongue running slowly
Between your breasts,
Around erect nipples
You're truly blessed,

Rising, falling
Slip 'n' slide,
Pulsating, throbbing
Deep inside,

Swaying, gliding
Rhythmic sighs,
Within the clench
Of quivering thighs,

The sound of love
Your glowing face,
Two bodies entwine

In sweet embrace.

Ashley O'Keefe

Lash!

The whip flicks against me
a sharp lashing tongue
that licks at my cold skin
the sting marbling the flesh
belying the inferno within,

that rages all the more
with each slap
each delicious bite,
molten lava pouring
out of me
as I writhe,
I surrender
there's no more fight.

The leather cracks
once more
I hold my breath as the whip sings
I want it harder
give me your all
I can take anything!

Lying here submitting
you push your way inside,
I scream your name as I climax,

Lash...
Lash...

Rawhide,

but my dark, dark eyes fix you
with a lustful gaze
from which you cannot hide,

for once you leave me sweating,
soaked through,
your desire spilt,
and me bruised and tenderised,

I'll still be gasping as I take control of that steaming whip,
and it's your turn to sweat
so get ready,
I'm an eager equestrian…
ready to ride!

Rhiannon Owens

It's A Dog's Life

Excited at being out of my cage
I bound forward enthusiastically.
She pulls my red lead and I slow to an obedient trot.
Proud in my studded collar,
I eagerly lap water from a metal bowl.
I gaze up lovingly and wag an imaginary tail.
Mistress rewards good submissive boys.

Rhiannon Owens

From Within Your Dreams

From within your dreams
Into this nightmare,
Opening your eyes
You're locked in his glare,

Thrusting, ramming
Poking the fire,
The heat, the sweat
His constant desire,

Your hands reach
Fingers clench,
You dare not scream
You heave, the stench,

Thrusting, ramming
Stoking the fire,
Your Incubus lover
Does he never tire?

Eyes tear with fear
Eyes peer with joy,
Eyes say "Don't fight"
They say "Enjoy".

Ashley O'Keefe

Pleasures Within

The more time I spend here
The less I want to return
I laugh exhilarated
Body tingling
I do not yearn
Here I burn
A glut of sensation
Climax
Then bliss
What on earth from that real world
Do you expect me to miss?
My desires, my hopes,
My dreams all unfurled.
My old life keeps falling
Further away
I'm so happy
I'm me
I smile every day
I gasp and I moan
Twist in ecstasy all night
Here, I'm desirable
I'm beautiful
Able to entice
Then delight.
Those shadows that linger
I kick them away
Too busy here
Loving
And being loved instead
I used to be stilted
But now I truly exist
Inside my own head

Rhiannon Owens

You (My Infatuation)

Wake, thinking of you,

Dreamt of you,

Head full of you,

You...

Rhiannon Owens

No Words

Gliding through hair
Caressing your face,
Kissing your smile
As fingertips trace,

The contours of you
Inhibitions stripping away,
Finger to lips, Sshh
There are no words to say,

Sliding along
The surface of your skin,
Finding myself
Deep inside, I'm within,

Controlling my urge
Satisfying your desire,
There's no turning back
Now we're on fire,

Faster and faster
The pleasure gets too much,
Exploding inside
Every feeling, every touch,

Quivering, shaking
So good, so intense,
Our glowing smiles
Feeling so immense.

Ashley O'Keefe

The Inner Realm

When my lines blur
and what seems real
is not,
when I wake from
that other realm
all perspiring,
so hot.

Feeling so dizzy
a smile on my lips,
running a nostalgic hand
down my swollen breasts,
my full-some hips.

Wondering which world
I now occupy,
my mind drifts
between the two,
gasping, here
with fingers inside me,

or floating
on buoyant waves,
as I'm filled brimful with you.

Heart pattering
in pained confusion,
which existence is real?
I remember
as soft sheets chafe,
my fingernails dig,
back arching
I ache,
with all the tortured yearning
I feel…

Rhiannon Owens

Trouble

When I listen to my head
It makes no sense at all,
When I listen to my heart
I get myself in trouble,
When I listen to my body
I get into trouble even more...

Rhiannon Owens

Your Smile

Into your dreams
My reaching hand,
"Take hold", I'll lift you
From the sand,

Sailing away
Toward the horizon,
To the real world
Dreams left behind you,

It's good to dream
Once in a while,
But life is too precious
Embrace it with your smile.

Ashley O'Keefe

Succubus (lies in wait)

Your Succubus lies in wait,
Knowing what she wants,
Pinning you between her thighs,
You're helpless as flesh starts to slide,
Silken, tongues and fingers glide,
She presses her mouth to you as she rides,
And you explode within her,
Deep into the slick, wet inside…

Rhiannon Owens

Within My Sleep

She haunts my dreams
Well, it's not really haunting,
Within my sleep
She's there, she's taunting,
Well, not so much taunting
More like flaunting,
If I'm not too careful
I'll surely be wanting,
And pretty soon
We'll both be jaunting,
Oh dear, oh my
It's all so daunting.

Aarrrrr...! Phew! I'm awake.

Okay, maybe another 10 minutes...

Ashley O'Keefe

One Hell of a Week (Seven Deadly Sins)

On **MONDAY** I was too proud,
they say it comes before a fall,

well…
I fell
straight down
to Hell,

On **TUESDAY** my greedy hands grasped,
grasped at what is mine…

This is mine!
That's mine too!
'What's yours is mine and what's mine is mine alone!'
My sole desire
is to acquire,

On **WEDNESDAY** I wanted you too, lusting:

Running my tongue over my lips
imagining you grasping me by the hips
pressing up close and hard
I need my fix
insatiable
wanting it all at once
to indulge, swallow you up
no measured sips,

THURSDAY I was envious, wanted what you had…

Envying you,
Begrudging you everything,
I'm petty

but it should be me, me, me…
and now the chips are down
yet still your friends rally round,
just so many glossy cherries
topping my jealousy,

On **FRIDAY**, I hungered…
Saliva dripping from my slack, seeking,
engorged mouth.
I'm groaning, gluttonous
cramming everything in.
"Feed me, feed me…"
still my belly rumbles,
it feels bad, it feels gooood - how can this be a sin?

SATURDAY… I angered…
I wish you could feel my wrath,
wish I could feel it too
so that instead of me being trodden on
people would walk all over you.
I can't seem to summon hatred
from my tired soul,
so I'll cut your vitriol from my life
and then I'll finally feel whole,

but, I was still angry…
There's no retribution today…
You're relieved,
But remember what they say
… About dishes when they're served cold
and how they're better that way!

Finally, a lazy **SUNDAY** afternoon, I slothfully stretch!

I reflect…

I could have been famous,
couldn't be bothered…

Nearly found love
but I stayed in bed…

Was writing a poem
but…

Rhiannon Owens

Dreams

In dreams
I am saved
By feelings of love,

In life
I am shunned, unneeded
Unloved,

In dreams
I am lifted to the sky,

Rescued, nurtured
Completely loved…

I fly.

Ashley O'Keefe

Entice

Each step I take
The rope doth shake,

Across the canyon
I soar, I quake,

I'm on thin ice
I feel the crack,

To you, I glide
No going back,

Skating along
I should think twice,

I fall, I sink
Your allure; entice.

Ashley O'Keefe

OLD AGE:

*The clocks are ticking
relentlessly, I lose time
yet life marches on...*

The Horizon

Old age was always a far-off place
On the horizon, over that hill,
Now it's creeping ever closer
I'm flying there, yet standing still,
My hair is becoming silver
(Well, maybe more like gold),
As I slowly close my eyes
Voices from the past unfold,
I hear the wit and the laughter
Recall those memories and good times,
But also the not so good
Friends and family lost in their prime,
I remember the innocence of childhood, the freedom of youth,
The responsibility of being an adult,
Getting married, my babie's first tooth,
Becoming a parent and a Grandparent (well not just yet)
It happens, it'll happen to you
So when you stare off toward the horizon
Just remember, one day... you'll get there too.

Ashley O'Keefe
(Live each day as if it's your last and never go to bed on an argument - Life is way too short)

168

Senior Moments…

NOT planning on going anywhere yet
DEAD is a long time to be
YET while there is breath in my body

I shall…

LIVE every second of each day fully
LOVE with all of this old heart of mine, and
LAUGH so hard that I pee!

"Not dead yet... Live, love, laugh"

Rhiannon Owens

When I Open My Mouth

I look in the mirror
What do I see?
My father there
Staring back at me,

I'm growing older
Feel the aches and pains,
Peering closer
See the wrinkles and veins,

I've noticed lately
There is no doubt,
When I open my mouth
My father comes out.

Ashley O'Keefe

Cruising

It isn't the Loveboat
nor a Ship of Dreams,
though there will be dancing
and a little bit of romancing,
but mainly just girls having fun…

Carol spent the first day hungover,
last night she really went to town
and today she's slumped in a sun lounger
with over-sized shades,
still in her crumpled cocktail gown.

She's on so many tablets
is Mary,
that she rattles as she walks
but she's been on the gin
so you can't hear the din,
it's drowned out by her slurred voice
as she talks and she talks,
with a lop-sided grin.
Rattle rattle
Prattle prattle
Rattling and prattling on!

Flo's there at every port in a storm
because she is a professional cruiser,
buying up and sourcing perfumes and designer clobber
to flog back home, in the local boozer.

Dolores was once a showgirl
and is a dab hand at flirting,
she's taken a shine to the Captain
and is glammed up to the nines every night

batting her carefully mascara-curled eyelashes,
he can't take his eyes off her
when she grabs at that mic…

Josie and Pat are at it again,
causing a ruckus in the duty-free
with Josie trying to wrestle packs of ciggies
from Pat's hands…
she's all protein shakes, health spa
and yoga you see!
Pat isn't taking this lying down,
she likes a smoke and she's having those fags,
things are starting to turn a bit nasty
and though Josie might be all fit and healthy,
Pat still packs a mean punch with her handbag.

There are plenty of eligible bachelors onboard,
and Sarah already has one ensnared,
he's rich and kind, and a gentleman,
all dapper and debonair.
His name is James,
he's her very own Bond
and she is having the time of her life,
she feels like she's floating on air
as he escorts her to the ballroom,
carefully steering her in her wheelchair.

They all love Annie to bits
but Annie likes her own space,
she's a culture-vulture soaking up
all the history, the art,
the architecture,
of each and every place.
She's the quietest of their group
but she fits in just fine,

with a wicked wit, and a sparkle in her eye
and some brilliant one-liners
as unexpected, as they are dry.

Barbara's been sad ever since her Eric passed
but has been chatting to a lovely man,
and it's heart-warming to see a smile on her face at last,
a flush to drawn cheeks, that were looking so wan.

It didn't take long for them to find their sea-legs
but now it's almost time to go home,
arms and suitcases loaded with pressies for the great-grandkids,
full of stories about the sea, the gentlemen, Sicily
and Rome.
Their children and grandchildren will scold them
because they never thought to phone them at all,
too absorbed on their little trip of a lifetime,
partying, loving, sunbathing…
basically just having a ball!

It wasn't the Loveboat
nor a Ship of Dreams,
though there was dancing
and a little bit of romancing…
it was just about girls having fun!

Rhiannon Owens

172

Strangers

Sitting here, waiting
Watching the door,
Who just came in
Who went out before,

A stranger walks in
She says she's my friend,
My wife? My daughter?
Their arms they extend,

This is my house
In here I am King,
Strangers want me gone
They say they're my kin,

Where are my family?
Where are my friends?
These strangers just haunt me
Into dead ends, I descend,

I'm frightened, I'm confused
I'm silent, I roar,
I just can't remember
What I came here for,

Listening to voices
I don't recognise,
Seeing their evil
It's in their eyes,

I'm frightened, I'm confused
I'm silent, I roar,
I just can't remember

Who I am anymore.

Ashley O'Keefe
(Inspired by the film - 'The Father' starring Anthony Hopkins).

Face Time

A face...
A map of wrinkles,
Tells a story over time,

Eye lines...
Tell of laughter,
The smiles of warm sunshine,

A forehead...
Of past worries,
The winters here and gone,

Engrained...
The roads of travel,
Across decades, the loneliness echoes on.

Ashley O'Keefe

Bring Me Sunshine

The Postman walked up the path to number 8, whistling a cheery tune. This was his favourite delivery of the day - he always left it till last and he always rang the doorbell, even if there were no letters for her!

He beamed as she answered the door. Piercing blue eyes met his, "Come on then soft lad," said Edie "Kettle's on - don't stand on ceremony!" and her sweet face lit up with her beautiful, crooked smile. The Postman followed her into the cosy living room and eased himself into a spotlessly clean, overstuffed armchair, eagerly anticipating a cuppa and a few custard creams.

"Treat for you today love," Edie said, shuffling in with a tray, "Bit of scouse for yer, get some meat on those bones."
He smiled and thanked her, she was always chiding him in a motherly way about being so thin. That was the first thing she'd ever said to him "You need a good pan of scouse down you."

Edie, 92 years of age and full of warmth and wisdom. The first time she invited him in for a brew he had sat taking in his surroundings. Mahogany furniture, a floral China tea set, lace doilies, net curtains, a patterned carpet. The constant tick-tocking of many clocks that should have been irritating but were actually rather comforting. He loved the cuckoo clock especially. He felt at home here. She would always say "I was vintage before it was trendy," and smile ruefully at him.

There was an old photograph of Edie and her husband dancing in the ballroom at Blackpool. "You should have seen us, we were smashing dancers. Ah, lad it's too late for me now, but you're still young enough to find love."

She traced her finger lovingly across the picture with a secret smile playing across her lips "I was lucky. I haven't the heart to start over now... and
besides, my Albert's always here with me anyway."

She spoke of them taking the ferry and spending time in New Brighton, and of their holidays in Morecambe, and how they danced. Always dancing. "Hey, remember Morecambe and Wise on the telly?" The Postman nodded and smiled, then began to whistle. Edie nodded along smiling wider and wider, then gave voice to the tune...

"Bring me sunshine, in your smile
Bring me laughter, all the while..."

Rhiannon Owens

After the Rains

Memories of our yesterdays
The hopes of our tomorrows,
The joys of the sun after the rains
The pains of all our sorrows,

Life and all its meanings
When all our work is done,
Life goes on with or without us
Our songs may or may not be sung,

Let's sail off into the sunset
Let's drift on calming seas,
Glide over life's vast oceans
On a clear sky tranquil breeze.

Ashley O'Keefe

Fading (Away)

Fading photographs
Won't erase you from my mind,
All I need are the memories
And the dreams to help remind,

This cruel disease won't beat me
I won't let it take you away,
I'll remember you forever
Until my dying day.

Ashley O'Keefe

MENTAL HEALTH:

Trapped

Locked within my own
Darkest imagination
Fighting to break free

Looking from the Inside

"I am not worthy...
I am not enough..."

Gently ROCKING back and forth
CHANTING to myself,
PULLING, RIPPING at my hair
I've tufts upon the shelf,

Through the frosted window
The moon reflects on me,
In its spotlight I am visible
The darkness can see me,

"I am not worthy...
I am not enough..."

Those shadows have appeared
In the silence of my mind,
They cackle and they echo
No peace am I to find,

From the outside I look crazy
From the outside; insane
But looking from the inside
All I feel is the pain,

"I am not worthy...
I am not enough..."

Ashley O'Keefe

Digging Deep

I dig my nails into my flesh
and I smile
though really it's a grimace
nails digging deep
blood beginning to pool
people ask if I'm okay
and I nod and smile at them
smile at you
while my fingers grip and claw
under the secrets of my sleeves
I smile and smile
grimacing jaws aching
I'm okay
I'm okay
mouth stretching wide
forced rictus grin
I'm okay
nails pinch rake scrape gouge.

Rhiannon Owens

Sound of Echoes

Below the ice
Pounding, heart beating,
The sound of echoes
Ice creaking, water seeping,

The world above
My world below,
The sound of cracking
My tears, don't show,

Sunlight through ice
Streaming through the dark,
Within its depths
It's left its mark,

The blinding sun
It's dizzy, it's golden,
I'm trapped, can't see
In a world that is frozen,

Below, I'm drowning
In the dark, unseen,
Gasping for air
No self-esteem,

Above the ice
I could never exist,
Below, my life's
A muffled watery mist,

I hear the laughing
From up above,
The sound of echoes...
The sound of love.

Ashley O'Keefe
(Inspired by 'Frozen Glass' by Rhiannon Owens, a poem from our book
Rhianno & Asley: A Voyage of Poetic Discoveries)

For You

I've never been pretty
but still try to dress like I am
for myself I thought,
but suspect it's for you.
Some years have passed
there are scars and flesh.
I have them
and you have them too.

Still, what do they have
the nearly naked,
purring, ego girls online?
Don't you remember my treasures
the jewels that are mine?

I still long for you,
yearn for that secret touch
in those places that delight.
I don't think I ask for much.

I lie here fretting
when I should be asleep,
cold where your arms don't hold me
and cold the tears that I weep.

Rhiannon Owens

On the Surface

Above with grace
And serenity,
Below like the cogs
Of industry,

Above like ballet
Upon a lake,
Below the paddles
For Titanic's sake,

Above like an Angel
Unfurling wings,
Below like Satan
With fork tail stings,

Above the white swan
Sailing by,
Below, webbed feet
Underwater… fly.

Ashley O'Keefe

Reflecting

Looking in the mirror
and I don't like what I see
staring back at me.
I see the personification of Dorian Grey's portrait,
an ugliness all-encompassing
if my eyes are the mirror to my soul
then my soul is empty

tarnished and black.
I want to smash this mirror
destroy this sickening visage
I grab it and shake it from side-to-side
hoping for something amazing,
for a kaleidoscopic miracle
but it's still me, ugly inside and out.
Self-absorbed rather than selfish
but when does my self-obsession become selfish
and the empathy I had become apathy?
Always the guilt, drowning in guilt
Good day = Guilt
Bad day = Guilt.
People say how can you be depressed
nothing bad has happened to you
or, if you dislike yourself
sort out your hair, your eyebrows, lose weight.
This loathing slams into my brain like a sledgehammer
no domino effect to release the blackness
just a grey wall that bears the brunt
and sends negative, distressing shockwaves
through my miserable body.
There's nothing behind my eyes
I pound at the mirror
bloody fists smashing in my own face
hoping to see something
anything

Rhiannon Owens

Invisible Scars

Broken internally
The invisible scars,
Exposed on the inside
On the outside, like Renoirs,

Her pain doesn't show
No one knows, no one cares,
It's her and her alone
On her own to say her prayers,

Feeling less than nothing
Looked on with contempt,
Shattered and shunned
In her life she's exempt,

In this depressive state
Her body cages her soul,
Hiding behind the shadows
Within her darkest hole.

Ashley O'Keefe

Identity

Staring out of the window into the starlight
at the me staring back from the other side,
a world between us, somewhere out there
like that mouse Fievel and his sister.

On one side is 'home' where I haven't yet managed to make
friends,
no identity forged for myself, I'm an alien.

On the other is 'home' where I'm in the way,
people have moved on, and changed
and I have stayed still and become stagnant.

The great divide.
The rising train fares.
Visits becoming less and less frequent.

Like Shirley Valentine said, I've lived such a little life.

Not much in common with anyone,
wondering where I fit
(if anywhere)?

Nobody remembers me...
Nobody knows me...
One side is safe and full of comfort and memories,
and people talk funny like me,

the other side is still unknown, and people talk funny but a
different funny than me...

but it also has you, and your arms,
where you will take me in your arms,

I will be in your arms,
I can be me in your arms,
at home in your arms.

Rhiannon Owens

Mummy's Tomb

Exhausted and naked
She stands in the shower,
Gently shedding those tears
'Cause the water flows louder,

Hiding in the bathroom
Her sanctuary, her solace,
The tears, they continue
If only she was aweless,

Feeling so tired
Like she can't go on,
What she would give
To be confident and strong,

She cries in her room
In an empty house,
Letting go in that moment
No more the quiet mouse,

She wants to feel pretty
She wants to feel slim,
She's no time to eat healthily
She's no time for the gym,

Her life is her family
She does all she can,
She's there for her children
She works for her man,

She feels unimportant
She feels of no worth,
Never feels she's enough
Only here to give birth,

She feels so alone
In that crowded room,
No life, just existence
Trapped in her own Mummy's Tomb.

Ashley O'Keefe

Voice

White noise in my head,
it's so hard to concentrate
as it builds and builds in volume,
a constant sound that grates.

It morphs into a chattering,
a cacophony of sound
like voices all overlaid,
I grip my temples, as my head pounds.

A stream of chanting,
it's hard to hear anything else
and the sound gains clarity,
all vitriolic words against myself.

Bitch, useless slag,
fat, ugly whore...
they tell me it would be better
if I wasn't here at all.

I can't make them stop
they are constant, won't leave me alone,
drowning out everything else
these voices I hear that are my own.

Rhiannon Owens

Thoughts

Thoughts scatter, unfocus
A mind in fear,
Locked away with the demons
Knife-like claws appear,
Stressed and afraid
Hiding away in the dark,
Making no sound
But ready to bark,
Those monsters appear
Shadows from the past,
Oh, to hush those fears
And find inner peace at last.

Ashley O'Keefe

Catch Me, I'm Falling

Is that you calling me?
Your voice I can hear?
It seems to be coming from far away,
Yet I sense you are near.

I'm falling
Spiralling,
Down
Down…
Pivoting, turning
Twisting
Into the sucking whirlpool
Of the abyss,
Where I will surely drown.

Down
Down…
Eyes squeezed shut tight,
Knowing that now the end is in sight.
Someone catch me I'm falling
And I don't know how or why,
I'm screaming soundlessly into the abyss,
Falling when I need to fly.

You caught me!
I'm okay,
And you never even knew.
You made me plant my feet back down
Just by being you.

I'm a survivor,
More… I'm living each day,
Because your simple, honest kindness
Helped keep the shadows at bay.

Rhiannon Owens

In the Moment

Out of the shadows
Into the light,
Mindful and focused
Winning this fight,

Those feelings and thoughts
Distant memories of the past,
Are now out of my mind
I'm free of them at last,

Living in the moment
To the future I glance,
No more stress, no more worries
I can finally take a stance.

Ashley O'Keefe

Sweet Thoughts

Tripping along in my own clumsy bubble,
thinking my own merry thoughts
of romance, adventure and sweet things,
existing where hope springs eternal
and I bask in the gentle sunshine of that spring.

I dream, I love, I live
with so much of my love to give,
and dark thoughts are kept at bay
because nobody can steal my thoughts from me,
and this place is mine,
private and sacrosanct
so I shall do things my way.

A little bounce to my step,
smiling from afar
singing my song,
dancing my crazy dance
to the erratic beating of my heart,
still swelling with that buccaneering spirit
and feelings of romance...

while the stars in my eyes are beaming
and I flicker with my own sweet light,
and sometimes I find my feet have left the ground,

as first I float
then I shoot through the clouds,
exploring rainbow and cloud
I take flight.

My own little bubble protects me,
I trundle onward
with a bounce to my step
and a tilt to my blushing lips,
and sometimes I strut
with defiance
though people may stare,
with a cheeky swing of my broad hips...

because nobody can steal my thoughts from me
and nobody can bar them
nor tax them,
my thoughts are honest
and pure and free
to circle and tease
and gain momentum,
existing in their own
eternal vibrancy.

Rhiannon Owens

Shining Armour

Part 1: SCATTERED

Her dreams float all around her
scattered like gentle feathers
from an angel's wing,
and she finds them hard to grasp
ephemeral fleeting kisses
that brush her fevered face,
they are like scenes in moving pictures
but she can't find a happy ending,
and already her skin grows cold
as the dark draws in,

She must needs find a new knight
so they can sing songs of love together,
and as she searches and searches
her eyes are half-blind
because there are no stars to light up the sky,
but she glimpses figures
shadowy phantoms
and she runs to catch up,
but they are always just out of reach...

'Are you he?' her voice rings out
like a bell through the night,
pleading
and she grasps one of the men,
he turns
and suddenly there is the light
from a blood moon,
and it lights up his twisted, deformed features
and the others all turn as one
with the same lascivious mutated faces,

If this were a fairytale she would swoon,
if it were a film her hero would save the day,
too late she is dimly aware of her shabby armour
as her horse gallops away in the night,
and they clutch at her garments laughing
as she gazes at what might have been
but could not,
wondering why he had to go away.

Part 2: GATHERED

From a nightmare she wakes
and gazes down at her torn and bloodied tunic,
heart numb
she can't even cry.

Footsteps approach,
and she gazes up at him
'Why did you leave me?'
and he shushes her,
shakes his head gently,

'You still don't get it do you?'
He holds out his hand
and helps her to her feet,
'I never left at all'
he says, as she stands on shaky legs,
'I watched over you,
through the dark...

... but don't you see?
It was not me who chased
those monsters away...
it was you!'

She looks down
at her white, unblemished gown
with a kind of wonder in her eyes,
'Oh,' she says,
'well, seeing as you are here anyway...
shall we dance?'

and they do,
laughing as the sun rises
and her hair streams out
beneath her floral crown,
and not a monster to be seen
because she chased them away.

Rhiannon Owens

Sunshiny Day

Sshh...
Gently tiptoe,

Away from the shadow
Move into the light,

Sshh now
Be careful,
We don't want a fight,

Ever so gently
Creep slowly away,
Away from the darkness
Into your sunshiny day.

Ashley O'Keefe

Whiteout

A place to hide
to be lost,
where I can never be found

A place where Horrors and shadows abound,
but there is nothing in my head,
I don't notice what surrounds
and my tears disappear
slipping down quietly,
without a sound

Whiteout
Whiteout

Nobody to hear my silent scream,
my voiceless shout

A headful of white noise
empty
but the silence deafens and pounds,
I'm lost
but I've little interest in being found

Whiteout
Whiteout

If only I could scream
but there's nothing left to let out

Nothing left
my thoughts blink out

Whiteout...

Rhiannon Owens

LOSS/SORROW:

Suffer in silence
A young, lonely heart breaking...
Life has no meaning

Two poems showing different points of view: -

Trapped (POV 1)

I came to you
With an open heart,
You're my only hope
My brand-new start,
After losing my Mother
My only friend,
She fought for her life
She fought 'til the end,
Now I have you
Who counts all my bread slices,
Who tots up my cost
Looks at all the prices,
You think my crying's controlling
And with my sadness, I seek,
Attention from you
I lost my Mother last week,
Every day you glare at me
And kill me inside,
With those uncaring eyes
You watch me sob, not confide,
I know I'm your hatred
I know I'm your rage,
How will I get through this
Trapped with you in your cage.

Ashley O'Keefe

Trapped (POV 2)

You came to me
With your open heart,
I'm your only hope
Your brand-new start,
After losing your Mother
My best friend,
She fought for her life
She fought 'til the end,
Now you have me
I can't afford the bread slices,
I have to count the cost
To look up the prices,
When you cry, I feel awkward
When you're sad, I feel weak,
I want to catch 'round you
I know it's loving you seek,
Every day I look at you
And feel your pain,
I do really care
But my tears I contain,
You must really hate me
You must feel afraid,
But we will get through this
Next week I get paid.

Ashley O'Keefe

In Dreams

Looking out across the river
the breeze lifting my hair
with gentle fingers
that bring back memories,
tears swim in my eyes,
the pristine waters blur

Carried away in my head,
the tilt of your chin, a knowing look,
the laughter we shared,
arch of an eyebrow
as you parted the smooth waters,
without a care

My eyes flit across the horizon,
seeking silhouette or shadow
but are you still there?

Looking back from bridge to treeline
I see the sun shine through your golden hair
Now long gone my presence still lingers
As you walk along the thoroughfare

Once we kissed on that very structure
As I stared into your emerald eyes
Parted lips my kisses lingered
We never said our last goodbyes

Your laughter lilting like weir bound waters
Cascading down into the stream
I am now a shade strolling this quarter
But still I visit in your dreams…

In your feverish dreams
you speak my name,
our names are like sighs upon
the whispering breeze

As the cool waters stream
I'm calling to you,
they stream my tears
of yearning,
of longing
and in your dreams,
the river calls to you too...

Rhiannon Owens & Carl Butler

No Longer Alone?

I catch her eye, sitting at the hotel bar. Light illuminates her face,
hair gleams, glass sparkles. We talk. Connect.

Tumbled in sheets, sweat drips, sighs are exhaled. I've been so
lonely. Dare I ask her to dinner?

She dresses. The money? Oh! Fumbling for the notes, head
hanging low.

Rhiannon Owens

Home of the Soul

A body empty of emotion
Unfeeling yet feeling free,
Soulless eyes, no more passion for life
Lie there staring back at me…

… Dead eyes, cloudy grey
Gaze into the mist,
Blind to life and its existence
Beyond the light, there is a twist,

My spirit travels freely
Interacting with the earth,
Through conscious communication
From the home of the soul, rebirth.

Ashley O'Keefe

Her Welcoming Smile (Mercy)

A Mother, a Sister
A best friend to all,
Her welcoming smile
When you came round to call,

*Now no longer allowed to work
'Limited leave to remain' expired,
A cruel system, a piece of paper
Refugees and migrants not rehired,*

Mercy, Mercy
A Mother and her child,
Alone, neglected
A Mother's soul, defiled,

Now no longer allowed to work
'Limited leave to remain' expired,
A cruel system, a piece of paper
Refugees and migrants not rehired,

Beside his Mother
Her baby boy cries,
Weakened by starvation
Swatting the flies,

Now no longer allowed to work
'Limited leave to remain' expired,
A cruel system, a piece of paper
Refugees and migrants not rehired,

Left functionally destitute
Let down by the system,
Left to go hungry
Let down, left a victim,

Now no longer allowed to work
'Limited leave to remain' expired,
A cruel system, a piece of paper
Refugees and migrants not rehired,

Left to the charities
To pick up the pieces,
Not 'a drain on society'
Now high priority: as she lies in her faeces,

Mercy, Mercy
A Mother and her child,
Alone, neglected
A Mother's soul, defiled,

A Mother, a Sister
A best friend to all,
Her welcoming smile
When you came round to call.

Ashley O'Keefe
(Inspired by Mercy Baguma from Uganda: A Mother 'found dead beside her baby boy' in a Glasgow flat)

Mother's Calling

I hear her voice
Though far away,
Sounding younger now
Than yesterday,

Slowly opening
My heavy eyes,
Tired of life
With all its lies,

I see my wife
With my daughter,
She smiles, she offers
A sip of water,

I try to say
"Mother's calling",
I think she knows
Smiling back, I'm falling,

Behind her smile
I see her pain,
For our daughter's sake

Holding back the rain,

A blinding light
A reaching hand,
Faint distant cries
As I leave this land,

Mother leads me
Into the light,
Where family wait
To reunite.

Ashley O'Keefe

Lost to the Shadows

Hands so frail, so cautious
Shaking gently out of reach,
Ashen in the sunlight
Greyish, ghostly, bleach,

Subdued and vulnerable
The sickness taken toll,
Fading into darkness
Reaching from a six-foot hole,

Withered over time
Worn down by the years,
Lost to the shadows
Life now disappears.

Ashley O'Keefe

Starlight

Gazing up at the ceiling
thinking of the night sky above
of the fathomless inky darkness
crying out for the radiance of love,

but my eyes close
and I find that I'm dreaming
of floating amongst the starlight
each star mesmerises

twinkling
beaming

and the moonbeams decorate my brow
and my heart is light
my silvered hair is streaming,
into a deep indigo bliss
pulled into a sweetly remembered kiss.

There is nothing bleak about the night-time
though it's cloaked in swirls of mystery
only morning sweeping away that cape,
but in the dawn's fierce glare,
our love is lit up brightly
with all of its flaws plain to see.

Rhiannon Owens

Her Innocence

Her innocence was dying
From the day that she was born,
Wrapped up in her blanket
All that comfort later torn,

Lost in the heat of lust
Scattered upon the floor,
Walked across and over
Just swept out the door,

The bloom within her cheeks
Hides the tear in her eye,
The countdown of her life
She cries behind the smile.

Ashley O'Keefe

Better Off

Gently rocking
Shrieking...

A rope taut
Creaking...

Staring at the floor
I sway and I drip,
A trickle down my leg
Tongue protruding over my lip,

I thought it would be easy
I thought it would be quick,

I struggled, suspended
In panic, I kick,

Drowning, choking
Gasping for air,
Burning eyes, purple-faced
Am I unaware?

How did I get here?
I just couldn't persist,
You're better off without me
I don't live, I exist.

Ashley O'Keefe

Winter's Sight

Traversing this endless vista
our numb fingers intertwined,
trees are crystallised
shimmering with ethereal light

If only you could see...

but the sharp, cold air
slaps our faces
with hard blunt kisses,
feverish kisses that burn

and the smell of decay
and rebirth fills the air

Snow has powdered your eyelashes,
dusted them

as I long to dust them with kisses,
your white lips smile toward me
and I yearn to
kiss them rosy again

Tiny intricate snowflakes
settle on my hand,
too exquisite to be caught
as perfect as you,
fleeting shards of joy,
transient
teasing
infuriating

If only you could see...

You catch them on your tongue
and your laughter is like pearls,
pearls of ice
smooth
and hard, and stinging

If only you could see...
If only you would see me...

Rhiannon Owens

The Sun's Pathway

Upon the shore
I stand and wait,
For the sun to appear
Through horizon's gate,

The salty smell
Of dawn's sweet breeze,
The sound of motion
Through rolling seas,

Across the water
Along its edge,
Light breaks the silence
Through sunshine's wedge,

Hues; peach and mango
The sky aglow,
Swimming the sun's pathway
Through the sea I go...

... Drifting, rolling, out to sea
No one sees the inner me.

Ashley O'Keefe

Lost Soul

My soul is lost
It searches for me...

My heart... it stops
Feeling... peaceably

Home to the lost
The lost one is me...

I am homeless, without
What is to become, and to be.

Ashley O'Keefe

Dancing for Eternity

There is the clatter of cutlery on delicate china,
the lively fizz of good champagne
and the gentle lapping of the water below them,
but Edie and Albert
only have eyes and ears for each other.

He takes her little hand in his
and puts it to his lips,
"You," he says softly
"Are every bit as beautiful
as the first day we met."
"When I was scrubbing the front step
with an old rag in my hair. You divvy!"
she exclaims, but a smile crinkles the corners of her eyes.
"Beautiful," he repeats,
and she blushes in spite of herself.

She reaches for the pretty teapot
but he stops her hand,
reaching across and filling her champagne flute
with the sharp fizzing liquid once again,
"I'm feeling very decadent" she says wryly,
and Albert replies *"Go ahead love - you treat yourself,*
God knows I'd spoil you if I could."
Their eyes meet once more,
"Sentimental old sod. I love you."
Albert stretches his hand out,
"May I have this dance?"
"Always..."

The other customers notice the elderly lady
who sits wearing a smart tea-dress,
a woman smiling a secret, crooked smile
her blue eyes shining,
as she gazes at an empty chair
that will never really be empty,

... She takes her Albert's hand
and they dance together on the elegant veranda,
the two of them framed by the beautiful sweeps and curves of the
art-deco building,

they dance on the shingled beach,
under an enchanted sky,
feet sweeping through the chill waters,

they dance and they dance
as they always will,
dancing
in their own
Happily Ever After!

Rhiannon Owens

The Sun will Shine Again

There are no words of comfort
Within a world of pain,
Loss rains in the heart
But the sun will shine again...

Loss is such a lonely place
But only for a while,
A place you feel an emptiness
A place, it's hard to smile,

A place of shock and numbness
A place of disbelief,
A place of pain and anger
A place amongst your grief,

But time is such a healer
Again the sun will shine,
As you travel up that rocky road
To the horizon, you will climb,

Your loved one, you'll remember
Your loved one, you won't forget,
And in time, with baby steps
You'll learn to live without regret,

There are no words of comfort
Within a world of pain,
Loss rains in the heart
But the sun will shine again...

Ashley O'Keefe

Talking with You

Old stone and stained glass
The sound of bells chime,
Then, the quiet, air tinctured
with the scent of incense and wine,

Candles, musty prayer books,
metal polish and flowers,
The silence, the sanctuary
Sitting in this pew here for hours,

Speaking with my Father
My Dad, not the Lord,
Times have been hard
I need his right-hand sword,

"Talking with you
Always took my fears away",
So here I am again
Listening to you, as I pray.

Ashley O'Keefe

Eternal

Above and beyond
On top of the world
Mountain peak through cloud,
A golden sun
Stars up high
Its beauty in a misty shroud,
Amongst a sea of white
Below a sky of blue,

Gazing into eternity
Life's timeless without you,
A place with no beginning
A place with no end,
Your face I see eternal
I miss your love, my friend.

Ashley O'Keefe

To Be with You

The sound of the river flowing
The sun shining through the trees,
The walk along the pathway
At the sight of you, I fall to my knees,

The thought of being with you
The talks, the holding hands,
The sitting here together
My silent pleas and quiet demands,

The river flows
The sun shines through,
I walk the pathway
To be with you...

Through my eyes, your face is glowing
How the time has flown,
As I sit here gazing at you
Through my tears, your face now stone.

Ashley O'Keefe

HOMELESS AND DRUG ABUSE:

Let Me In

Inside where it's warm
Full of love and safe shelter
To live a real life

High-Horse

They say that I am scum,
they call me a disgrace,
saying I'm 'out of it on spice'
saying I'm 'off my face'

Actually, I don't touch drugs
I just try to grab some sleep in the day
when people are near,
I'm a frightened woman on my own,
vulnerable, having to stay vigilant
because the nights are long and dark
when you live in constant fear

So I sleep on city streets
as the shoppers bustle on by,
my meagre belongings as a pillow,
taunted by scents of food I'll never taste,
as people try not to catch my eye

... and who could blame me if I was using,
to numb the loneliness and pain,
to block out the snide comments,
and the freezing sting of rain?

You are not so very far
from where I am now,
so remember that pride
comes before a fall,
and when you finally tumble
and lie broken on the floor,
a horse so incredibly high
is of no use to you at all.

Rhiannon Owens

Over the 'Bumps' We Go

A stifling sound...

A road stretches
Far off into the heat,

A straight path
To the horizon,

Along a heat haze street,

A highway through the desert
A car with a radio,

Turning up the music
Over the 'bumps' we go,

Snorting... Bumping...
Snorting 'bumps' of blow,
Along a highway through the desert
Over the 'bumps' we go,

Turning up the music
A car with a radio,
A highway through the desert
Over the 'bumps' we go.

Ashley O'Keefe

God-like Complex (Coked up!)

Let's refer to you as Zeus,
not because you are a Greek God,
but because you display
the arrogance of one!

Snorting your life away,
playing mind games...

You probably are a decent bloke
under the cocaine aggression,
and intelligent too...
but your superiority complex
and Jekyll and Hyde mood swings
are way out of proportion,
at odds with the red face,
spluttering cough, wheezing chest
and the stupid lamp-like
bloodshot eyes.

You use people,
lift them up so high
boosting their confidence
just to smash them into the ground...
the way your false high
hurls you heavily,
spiralling
into the bleakest of
comedowns…

Hoovering that shit up your nose,
addling your skewed brain
if it carries on
you'll end up,

one very
very
lonely man indeed.

Rhiannon Owens

Shadows

Shadow on the wall
A gun to the head,
No sound of a shot
The shadow drops dead,

Shadow on the wall
A sword to the neck,
No song from the blade
The head hits the deck,

Shadow on the wall
A needle is drawn,
The poison injected
A 'rush' 'til the dawn,

Shadow on the wall
The moon and the stars,
Away with the fairies
For a lifetime on Mars,

Shadow on the wall
A shadow of myself,
A shadow in darkness
Locked away in itself.

Ashley O'Keefe

When the Party is Over

Little Miss Fun
as deluded as they come
Little Miss Fun,
aged 41,
surrounds herself with youthful adulation,
then tries to put her adult head on,
because she is 41.

Little Miss Fun lives for drugs and partying,
always trying to pull the nearest man,
a sure indication her veneer
of good-time girl,
is an insecure sham.

Little Miss Fun thinks the chemicals open her mind,
they make her deep,
Little Miss Fun is another lost sheep.

Everything has become a pretension,
she's mixed up and lonely
with a constant need for attention.

She fills her home with her false little 'friends',
people who use her,
then laugh...
nasty scum,
I wonder if any will be there in the end?

Her real friends moved on,
the party ended long ago
but Little Miss Fun
parties on,
alone,

sinking further into despair
feeling so low.

Rhiannon Owens

We Must Cry

For the children of the streets, *we must cry*
To chemicals, they turn when love's run dry,

Feelings not granted when they were young
Now trapped, never-ending, death for some,

Needing money and the drug to survive
Addicted to that adrenaline feeling inside,

For the children of the streets, *we must cry*
They should never need to seek the drug that makes them high,

Feelings of real love are what they needed
To be brought up on love and hugs, their nurture heeded,

Now fallen prey to the lucrative and corrupt
Turned to crime and begging, their desperate hands cupped.

Ashley O'Keefe

Home

Quivering in the cold
in abject fear,
people send me on my way
kick me when I'm down,
they won't let me near,

I'm frightened and hungry
and all on my own,
you took me in one Christmas
long ago
but here I am all alone,

Please welcome me
into the warmth of your home,
give this old dog a chance…
please throw me a bone!

Rhiannon Owens

Seek the Stars

Through cloud, I seek the stars
All my spirit finally gone,
There was a time I had it all
Where did it all go wrong...?

Financial pressures finally
Pushed me to the brink,
Homelessness, depression
Into a cold hard world, I sink,

Devastating, dangerous
Living in isolation,
Alone on the streets
Amongst violence and frustration,

Mental health, drug misuse
I've had, I've done it all,
Through this life, over time
I broke, I trip, I fall,

As the sound of footsteps echo
Running down the street,
Lying here in the gutter
I'm soaked, I'm kicked, I'm beat,

Through cloud, I seek the stars
All my spirit finally gone,
Raindrops fill my eyes
Nevermore to see the dawn.

Ashley O'Keefe

One More Drop

Just one more drop
to numb the pain,
feelings become fuzzy-edged
but every day is the same,
guilty thoughts
just another drop
again,
no chance to change
erratic thoughts,

Face up to life,
what's to gain?
Stark reality,
racing thoughts
and every day the same,
everything too loud
everything too bright,
but you know you need to step into the light,

Time to face that reality,
however bleak
however much hatred
I have for me,
because if I don't
I might never make it back,
might drown in my own
alcoholic sea
of reckless behaviour,
stroke or heart attack,
or locked into my own senility,

Just one more drop,
after that...

I'll feel lots better
and then I swear I'll stop…

Rhiannon Owens

Under the Moon & the Stars

The Accordionist stands back-lit
by the light from a busy restaurant,
like his own spotlight
as he stands eyes closed,
swaying,
lost in the mournful
bittersweet notes of his music,

An Accordionist plays under the Moon and the Stars…

"Here you go fella," his eyes snap open
and he sees a man in threadbare clothing
drop fifty pence into his hat,
before shuffling on his way
with a lone carrier bag, holding a meal for one,

Still the Accordionist plays on,
the notes hauntingly beautiful
echoing through the night
as late shoppers and early revellers
walk on by,
with single-minded purpose,

A young couple approach,
cheeks flushed
a little tipsy,
wine on their breath

and smiling with delight in their eyes
the soft suffusion of love lighting their faces
they begin to dance,
close and soft
and sweet,
feeling as though they are in a street in Paris,

Un Accordéoniste jouant sous la Lune et les Étoiles...

He thinks perhaps they will spare a coin
but away they go,
still half-dancing
enraptured,
too caught up in each other,
he sighs...

but then she clutches at the arm of her beau,
swings round on an impulse
and runs back toward him,
hair whipping at those rosy-hued cheeks,
"Thank you", she says with an open smile,
proffering a five pound note that he tucks into his pocket,
the young man waves to him,

An Accordionist plays under the Moon and the Stars...

People pass by
the strains of music unappreciated,
a group of drunk scallies shouting, jeering
"Why don't you get a proper job... Your music's shit"
callous laughter bouncing around wall and pavement,

Un Accordéoniste jouant sous la Lune et les Étoiles...

He has finished for tonight

and he reclines in the doorway of a disused shop,
sheltered in his cardboard castle,
he holds his old accordion to him tenderly,
like the embrace of a gentle lover...
and he dreams of those young lovers
dancing through the streets of Paris,

As he plays his accordion under the Moon and the Stars...

Rhiannon Owens

LOVE:

*A symbol of love
forevermore... Roses red,
red roses galore*

You & Me

I think we knew from the beginning
It would always be you and me.
Half an hour or so of shyness
Then like it was meant to be.
We'd chatted for hours and hours
From a distance over the phone,
Already friends, the attraction was there
We would no longer be alone.

The past had burnt our fingers
And shut our emotions up tight,
But just being in each other's company
Was so different and so right!

It hasn't always been easy...
The distance and cashflow worry!
There've been tears and insecurities,
Silly things said in frustration and hurry...

... but with patience, respect and trust,
plus affection, cwtches and lust,
we strengthened the bond
that had always been there,
along with the happiness and laughter we share.

I learn from you,
and you learn from me,
we fit together so naturally!

Today we cement our relationship,
March forward together in life.
We'll continue to grow
and love one another,

but from now on
as husband and wife!

Rhiannon Owens

Hearts Collide

Skin burning
with mutual yearning,

Into each other's arms we return,
familiar contours to be relearned.

Hearts collide.
Smashing at our ribcages,
cushioned by our bodies.
Cupped inside.

Wrapped in skin and love
and love and skin.
Loving the skins we are in,
loving the secrets within.

Nobody owns us
but we belong to each other.
Drinking ourselves in.

We are two people
with two hearts,
but connected.

Where one ends
the other begins.

Rhiannon Owens

The Promise

Beneath the starry sky
Amid the wintry air,
And the beauty of the moon
Gazing gracefully with glowing stare,

Beneath the velvet blackness
As the moon and stars doth shine,
I give to thee a promise
My heart and soul be thine.

Ashley O'Keefe

Celestial Sphere

Face-to-face
Clothes slip down,
Silhouetted by moonlight
In a birthday gown,

Curvaceous bodies
Caressed by fingers,
Seductive, sensual
The moment lingers,

Into the darkness
Shadows disappear,
And moonlight shines
In a celestial sphere.

Ashley O'Keefe

It's Puzzling

I could never find the last jigsaw piece
somehow it always seemed to elude me
and I think that universities ought to
offer a Rubix cube degree.
Somewhere on the dot-to-dot
I'd go so very wrong
and playing Cluedo with someone like me
meant the game was tediously long.
One crossword space I could never fill
and always miles out on 'spot the ball'
each time something wrong or missing
I just couldn't complete a puzzle at all.

Then one day I found that last jigsaw piece
and it was the perfect fit
my ducks in a row on the Rubix cube
no longer baffled by life or by it.
I know who was in the conservatory
Professor Plum with the rope
and the dot-to-dot is a whole picture
I just made the final pencil stroke.
Now I'm completely 'on the ball'
and I've deciphered the final clue
it's your name that completes both crossword and me
my missing puzzle piece was you!

Rhiannon Owens

Always Been You

The warmness, the softness
The glow in your smile,
Every day is like Christmas
You make life worthwhile,

Loving you is so easy
It's like riding a bike,
We never forget
Or go to bed on a fight,

Life has been hard
With its ups and its downs,
Life's been a circus
And we've been the clowns,

I wouldn't change a thing
Well, maybe one or two,
But on the whole, I'm so glad
There's always been you.

Ashley O'Keefe

Love Me Still

Cross my lips,
not my palm, with silver,
give me golden words
not frankincense or myrrh.

Whisper to me,
sing our loving song
and remind me that,
you will always be there.

Smooth my furrowed brow,
like snakeskin, worries shed,
hold me tenderly in your arms,
plant sweet kisses upon my head.

Rhiannon Owens

Always My Song

To your gift
I'm the wrapping
On Christmas day,

But not just at Christmas
The bells always play,

Throughout the years
Winter's come, Winter's gone,
Summers and Springtime
You're always my song,

Now Autumn approaches
We've seen joys, we've had tears...

It's our time to embrace life
To catch hold... no fears.

Ashley O'Keefe

Because I Love You

If ever you wish I'd say what's on my mind,
If you wonder what I think about,
If you longed to be telepathic,
Any clairvoyant would tell you
(and you don't have to be one to guess!),
It's that I love you!

If you wonder who I love in the Autumn,
When we kick through the bright, fallen leaves.
If you wonder about it in the pureness of Spring,
The madness of March,
When my step is light,
And my heart is lighter.
If you knew who I cherish
on relaxed Summer days,
When the heat has made me lazy,
And it's too much of an effort to say.
Or who I'd snuggle up to in Winter,
To block out the wind and the rain,
To keep me close,
And warm,
It's you!

And I want to grow old with you,
Though I'd rather not grow old at all,
But I know I'll never feel old with you,
You'll keep me young,
Because I love you!

And now it's time to apologise,
For the bizarre things I say and I do,
But before I begin my ramblings,
Just remember that I love you.

I'm sorry for my extreme moods,
When I snap,
And when I argue,
Or when I'm down in the mouth,
I can't communicate to you,
That it's because I love you!
I'm sorry that I can be so completely happy,
That you'd be forgiven for suspecting drugs,
And I laugh,
I shout,
And I sing (out of tune),
Make (bad) jokes,
And do the most childish things,

But my only drug is you,
You make me feel so free,
Because I love you!

I'm sorry that sometimes,
I smile at you every two seconds,
Or I stare at you,
And like what I see,
Or into your eyes,
With a secret smile in my heart,
But it's because I love you!

I'm sorry that sometimes I cling,
Am reluctant to let you go,
And fuss like a Mother Hen,
Or demand to be fussed over,
When something's ruffled my feathers,
And I need them to be smoothed,
But it's only because I love you!

I'm sorry for all the crude remarks,

The risqué jokes,
And those blatantly suggestive comments,
But it's because I want you!

I'm sorry for my jealousy,
But it's because I can't have you!

And if you've never wondered what I'm thinking,
Or wanted to know,
And if you don't see any reason for my apologies,
It doesn't matter,
Because I love you!

Rhiannon Owens

Out of the Blue

Evening sunset
Morning dawn,
In and out like the tide
Across a sand summer lawn,

Feelings, emotions
Flying so high,
Riding those waves
All in the mind's eye,

A daydream, reverie
Thinking of you,
Lost in the moment...
Out of the blue.

Ashley O'Keefe

The Song Within Your Eyes

Within your eyes
A song of love,
It whispers
And it plays,

Across the floor
Is this a dream?
The rhythms
And the sways,

Slowly, sensual, closely dance
Covering the floor,
Gliding and surprising
Reaching out for more,

From Tango to Flamenco
The tempo starts to rise,
Into a frenzy so intense
The song within your eyes.

Ashley O'Keefe

Kilig (Butterflies in the Stomach)

Knotted tongue fumbles for words
I'm as dizzy as an awkward teenager
Looking down at my feet
Instead of in your eyes, that
Gleam bright with our hopes and desires

Rhiannon Owens

Picturesque

Road-like ripples
Across the sea
Toward the fury of the sun,

Morning's dawning
Seagulls calling
A new day has begun,

The horizon glows
Its pot of gold
Illuminates the sky,

Mango hues
Spread into blues
So pleasing on the eye,

On gentle breeze
Over glinting seas
The smell of salty air,

Upon the sand
You hold my hand
A picturesque affair.

Ashley O'Keefe

Heart & Soul

We found each other somehow
and I'm thankful every day,
this funny girl and boyo
who had sadly lost their way.
Connected heart, soul and mind
with a love that is rare to find,
so painfully honest
we can stand side-by-side.
From here on now,
there is a song of joy in my heart
for Rhiannon and Her Taff
have a brand new start.

Rhiannon Owens

Holding Tight

I've been waiting for such a long time
Such a long while for you,
Now you've come into my life
Into my heart, is it true?

The smile in your eyes doesn't tell any lies
When darkness surrounds, we're holding tight.

You've been waiting for such a long time
Such a long while for me,
Now I've come into your life
Into your heart, is it true?

The smile in your eyes doesn't tell any lies
The touch of your hand helps me understand,

The warmth of your lips makes me feel so sure
When darkness surrounds, we're holding tight.

We've been waiting for such a long time
Such a long while it's true,
Now we've come into our lives
Into our hearts, is it true?

The smile in our eyes doesn't tell any lies
The touch of our hands helps us understand,
The warmth of our lips makes us feel so sure
When darkness surrounds, we're holding tight.

Ashley O'Keefe

You Were There

The darkness tugs and pulls at me,
I struggle but I can't break free,
But then I sense that all might be right,
You're there leading me into the light.
I was all mixed up, feeling like nobody cared,
felt all alone but suddenly you were there.

Rhiannon Owens

The Clock Slowed

The high-pitched purring of the electric hedge-trimmer had come to an end as the front door opened. She stepped out, struggling with a suitcase.

Putting down the trimmer, I rushed over to help.
"I need time," she said, "time to think."
I could see it in her eyes. She was struggling with more than the suitcase…
… She's my world, I thought, choking up as I watched her drive away.

Waiting, waiting. The clock slowed.
I'd walk around the house, hands in my pockets, tears in my eyes.
I'd sit at the table, two places prepared.

We met up, we talked, laughed, cried. She was coming home.

With a spring in my step, the table set, the kettle on…
… Waiting, waiting.

She never came… the clock slowed.

Ashley O'Keefe

Dancing in The Rain

Us
Two,
Outside
In the rain,
Catching the cool drops
That fall plumply into our mouths,
Splashing through the muddy puddles with sweet joyous glee,
Kissing with saturated abandon as our brollies patiently bob by
wet feet!

Rhiannon Owens

We Fly

The healing power of love
Lights up the darkest sky,
Amongst the moon and stars
On beautiful wings we fly,

All through the night
Until the glinting light of dawn,
Into that emotional sunrise
Where two hearts have been drawn.

Ashley O'Keefe

Thunder Rock

As the sun sets on the horizon
As the seagulls fly up high,
I find myself at Thunder Rock
Looking up at the clear blue sky,
This day's been one to remember
I know you think so too,
It's the day I spent at Thunder Rock
It's the day I spent with you

We walked along the shoreline
We talked while holding hands,
We didn't need a bucket and spade
Building castles in the sand,
This day's been one to remember
I know you think so too,
It's the day I spent at Thunder Rock
It's the day I spent with you

Our time has passed so quickly
The night is drawing near,
The waves are crashing on the rocks
It's time that we weren't here,
This day's been one to remember
I know you think so too,
It's the day I spent at Thunder Rock
It's the day I spent with you.

Ashley O'Keefe

Fly Me to the Moon

Fly Me to the Moon
watch me light up
the sky,
a shining shooting star
twinkling with joy
as we play and ride
amongst comets and meteors,
frolicking way up high.

Fly Me to the Moon
brighten up this darkest night,
do it quickly do it soon
because the morning is in sight.

Watch the moonbeams
dance
across my smiling face,
with a sparkle in my eyes
of any lingering sadness, there's no trace.

Watch me shine
flaming, burning
with all my little soul
no more yearning,
no more longing
because I'm finally whole.

Fly Me to the Moon
where you are near
and not far,
the daylight is dimming my brilliance
can you catch a falling star?

Rhiannon Owens

I Have Loved

I have loved the stars too fondly
to be fearful of the night,
I lived my life in the shadows,
shrouded in darkness
but now I embrace the light,

I had my fingers burned too often
to be cowed by flames or fire,
these days I like to fan those flames
stoke my red-hot poker desire,

and I've no fear of the bite of thorns
of which the roses beauty doth conceal,
the drops of blood that dot my skin
remind me of what is real...

Reminded that my fate isn't sealed,
and that the cards I don't need
will not make the deal,
I laugh, I cry, I rage,
and above all, I feel...

I'm not afraid of flying,
I'll fly so very high
because I got sick of falling
so now I take to the skies,

I'm never frightened of the waves,
upon the turbulent sea
and I'll not be seduced by sirens,
I'm immune to their treachery...

because their song might lure in the weak,
the broken,
those who feel alone...
but their singing evokes no emotion in me,

I sing out loud and clear - the sweetest of songs,
a song of my very own!

The monsters under my bed
do not disturb my sleep,
I've battled the demons within me,
I was scarred, they'd bitten deep…
demons that would make
the most formidable monster weep!

I've cried too many tears
for my spirit to be doused by the pouring rain,
my tongue seeks, catches,
mouth tasting the bitter drops,
cool liquid refreshes, salving my pain,

Spinning, twirling,
dancing in the rain
laughing deliriously,
I found myself again…

I'm not afraid of anything!
You helped me, now I soar,
I learned to feel, I learned to love
and to love myself most of all.

Rhiannon Owens

250

Silk and Feathers

Slipping the straps from your shoulders
Slowly sliding down your arms,

Leisurely revealing...
Your beautiful charms

Suddenly falling...
Dropping to the floor

Silk at your feet,
Revealing even more,

Shifting your hair,
Long flowing to one side

Softly kissing your neck,
At the back and on the side

Gently catching around you
Holding you near,
Whispering sweet nothings
Into your ear,

Revolving, spinning
Turning around,
We are dancing like doves
Sharing lips, we are bound,

Dancing on and on
Then we dance on some more
We fly, we glide,
We're eagles...

As one, our feathers soar.

Ashley O'Keefe

MISCELLANEOUS:

Beyond the Shore (Waves)

*Stars, dreams and dancing,
poems swell this ocean of
endless inky words...*

Solitude

An inner peace, a quiet grace
A feeling deep inside,
In solitude, you're not alone
Your whole being calms the tide,
Inner confidence, self-belief
Reliance on yourself,
Both the teacher and the master
The book of wisdom on the shelf.

Ashley O'Keefe

The Day the Night Did Not End

The sky is black as jet
Not a star
To mar
Its dark obsidian
Not a star to be seen
In this vast expanse
Just the interminable
Darkness
The darkness
The darkness abounds…

Lying in bed
Waiting for the dawn
For the daylight
To penetrate
The birds to trill
Their song
Of morning
The morning
Morning dawning
With its familiar sounds …

The dawn never comes
Gazing out
Of the window
Searching for a
Speck of light in the darkness
And still
Not one star
A star
Not one little star
Can be found…

For this is the day
That the darkness
Never went away
And no daylight
The daylight
Daylight
Was never seen again
Though we never
Stopped believing
The day would
Come around.

(way up above
through time and space
far in the distance
glowing weakly at first
a tiny star starts to shimmer
but shining brighter
with persistence
a tiny catalyst
a little spark
holding up a match
to hope's flickering glimmer)

Rhiannon Owens

Until Morning

Wrapped in its blanket
Wrapped in its cloak,
Under cover of darkness
Asleep, I awoke,

At rest in my slumber
In dreams I awake,
And fly above rooftops
Reality I forsake,

In my lucid dreams
I'm clearly aware,
And in full control
Until morning comes to bear,

To awake in the real world
From the dark into light,
I'd escaped for a moment
How I long for the night.

Ashley O'Keefe

When the Lights Go Out

The storm has caused a power cut
in homes across the nation
suddenly families everywhere
have to revert to the art of conversation.
The television's on the blink
and the Internet is down
does the idea of communication
sound good, or cause us all to frown?

A married couple sit in the dark
will this allow them to reconnect
will they get to know each other all over again
or is it time to press eject?
Will they giggle as they bump into each other
and take a spontaneous delight
making sensuous love in the flickering shadows
of torch or candlelight?

Could this be a whole new chapter
a new appreciation of one another
remembering all they've shared
a rich tapestry woven by lovers?
Or has this shown their estrangement
that it's time to draw a line?
We'll never know, the lights are back on
'Stick the telly on love, and pass us the wine!'

Rhiannon Owens

On Their Way

By lorry or boat
They run, they hide,
For a better life
They swim the tide,

Life or death
It's worth the risk,
Together with family
They must be brisk,

Refugees -
Forced to flee,
Persecution -
And austerity,

Dead or alive
Washing up on our shores,
Hoping for help
Seeking open doors,

Living in fear
If they go, if they stay,
At the toss of a coin
They're on their way.

Ashley O'Keefe

Lighthouse

The lighthouse
Bathed in coastal air,
Of rain and brine
A salty affair,

Standing tall
At the end of a quay,
Where fishermen cast
Their lines out to sea,

Once gaily painted
In black and white,
Now pitted walls
A rubbish site,

Worn with time
And storms of fear,
Now graffitied
'Take rubbish home, KEEP CLEAR'.

Ashley O'Keefe

A Confusing Mass of Words

Who invented words for words?
Who invented the word, word?
Who invented who?
And who invented, invented?
How was and invented?
And how was, was made?
How was made created?
And how was how invented?
Who invented created?
And why, and when, and how?

Oh! Is all my life going to be,
Such a confusing mass of words?

Rhiannon Owens

Gathering Dust

Stories and chapters
The memories of pain,
So deep and emotional
Almost drove me insane,

They've been locked away
For all of these years,
Gathering the dust
Now empty shelves are my fears,

Those books have been sprawled
All over the place,
Now I must relive
All those demons to face.

Ashley O'Keefe

Alternate Strokes

Alternate strokes
Alternate sides,
Pulling the blades
Through water; glides,

Quiet waters
Tranquil, still,
The sun breaks through
The morning chill,

Alternate strokes
Alternate sides,
Pulling the blades
Through water; glides,

Stroking through water
Out of the mist,
Travelling the river
I float, sun-kissed,

Alternate strokes
Alternate sides,
Pulling the blades
Through water; glides,

Seated, paddling,
Double-bladed,
Trees overhang
I'm covered; shaded,

Alternate strokes
Alternate sides,
Pulling the blades
Through water; glides.

Ashley O'Keefe

Bones

Pillow-talk, he's opening up to you
in the sleepy aftermath,
post-coital bliss
but there's a rattling coming from inside the cupboard

Rattle Rattle Rattle

A thumping at the door.
How does he not hear it?
For God's sake, can't he shut up!
All this over-sharing,
my brain can't take all this noise

Chatter Rattle
Blah Blah
Rattle
Rattle

Can't focus, he's wittering on
and on, and on…
the rattling is louder
and now…
Bang
Bang Bang

Something trying to get out.
I scream and scream
hands tearing at my hair

Scream
Screaming

'Shut up, shut up…
SHUT UP!…'

and finally he has

but I'm babbling incoherently,
shrieking out words that
spill over one another
in my haste to spit them out,
and all the time the rattling
the banging on the door

Rattle Rattle
Bang Bang Bang
Bang Bang
Rattle

… and I'm screaming the words at my partner
as the door smashes open
and all of those skeletons in my closet
collapse on top of me,
burying me,
with their bony condemnation
entombing me,
but exposing my sins

So many skeletons in my closet
they were always going to come tumbling out,
grinning with malicious glee
as love walks out on me,
broken-hearted,
leaving me
just a pile of broken bones,
crying into the debris of my own darkest deeds

Crashing
Banging
Rattling
Shrieking…

Rhiannon Owens

Alive or Dead

Driving along
There's something up ahead,
Lying in the road
Is it alive or is it dead?

As I get closer
She rolls into the gutter,
Trying hard to stand
Through my window, I hear her mutter,

Picking up the lady
She'd fallen and banged her head,
Thinking she was dazed or shocked
But she was drunk instead,

I asked to call an ambulance
To which she did reply,
"What's the point, I'm always drunk,
Only call them when I die".

Ashley O'Keefe

Along Life's Road

'Splish' through the puddle
A revolving wheel,
The cattle grid 'cackle'
A juddering feel,
The 'beep' of the horn
As we drive around the bend,
The 'creak' of the tree
Along life's road we ascend.

Ashley O'Keefe

The Incessant Rain

Snuggled into the armchair
on this cold and rainy night,
a book set upon my lap
where normally the cat would curl.
Rain streams down the window
Pitter-patter pitter-patter
a steady stream.
Hypnotic that sound, almost rhythmic,
lulls me at first
but then starts to set my nerves a jingle
Pitter-patter pitter-patter.

Raindrops bouncing off the glass.
Oh, this incessant rain!

I worry about my newly planted bulbs,
wonder if the rain will wash away the virgin earth,
exposing their vulnerability
their paper-thin skins.
Drowning them before they ever see the daylight again.
No flowers this spring.
What else might the rain uncover?
Soil swirling away to reveal human remains,
bleached skeletal bones glinting in the sickly moonlight.
At this very moment is the owl ripping the very flesh,
from around the still beating heart of its prey?
While the raven watches on
from the twisted, deformed branches
of the blackened, gnarly tree,
his heart even blacker
his eyes full of malice.

Pitter-patter pitter-patter
I worry I will hear the *drip drip drip*
of the ceiling beginning to leak.
Wait!.. Is that a face at the window

staring in at me?
Or just a distorted jumble
of rain and shadow 'pon the glass?
Is it merely the twisted outline
of the twisted boughs
on the twisted tree
waving madly at me?
Or the spindly arms of some snarling, nocturnal beast?

Safe in my cocoon,
and everything so silent, so still
save for the steady beat of the rain.
The pulsing, beating heart of the heavens.
The house is slumbering,
I would think I were alone
and where is the cat?
No fleeting sound of mouse
in earnest quest for some scrap or crumb.
Is it more frightening to be all alone,
or to fear that which creeps in the shadows?
... and there again that face at the window.
Could it be my own pitiful reflection,
pinched and pale gazing back at me,
and those blanched bones
those smooth, white bones
surely a figment of my imagination?
Just the wan moon reflected in the dismal, muddy puddles.
All reflections I reflect.

Now branches scrape the window
... or those emaciated arms again.
The fiend, the fiendish fiend!
God! The rain.
Now the noise becomes a drill
nay, a drum!
A constant *thud thud thud*
shredding my raw nerves,
worrying my feverish mind.

There it is again!
That hated face!
That hideous visage!

I cup my shaking hands
around a glass of red wine.
Sweat drips down my face
drip drip drip
incessant like the rain,
pooling in the wine in little, oily swirls
... like blood,
crack in the glass like a vein
wine spreads and reaches out for me,
swirls of red red red
I smash the glass down onto the table
and it shatters.
Jagged veins, oozing blood
my reflection over and over,
terror in my eyes.

drip drip drip
thud thud thud
Where is the cat?
Sweat drips down my face,
incessant like the rain

Where is the cat?
Oh! When will the rain stop?
Will it ever stop?
What if it never stops
never ceases...
Nevermore!

Is there anybody there
out in the rain,
or am I all alone?
Trapped in this house,
suffocating in this mausoleum of my own making,

as the diabolical rain
and its monsters, the demon eyes close in around me.
That ghastly face
that hellish beast!
... but no no no
a reflection
only my reflection, nothing more
trick of the light.
Perhaps the Edgar Allan Poe book
was a bad idea
in hindsight
and the wine...

but can this night never end
won't this pounding in my head cease
the beating of my hideous heart?
God! The rain the rain
my feverish mind and its macabre imaginings.
Sweat drips down my face
incessant like the rain

pitter-patter pitter-patter

There is something at the window.
There is nothing at the window
staring in at me

drip drip drip
but what if...
thud thud thud

Perhaps I should close the curtain
shut out the night and its thousand eyes
thud thud thud

staring in at me.

Shouldn't be reading the Edgar Allan Poe

his devilish works!
The wine hasn't helped.
Where, oh where is the cat?

Rhiannon Owens

BEYOND DREAMS:

In Poetic Dreams

Out at sea, stars gleam
We travelled further than seemed...
Way beyond our dreams

Fading

Sometimes I worry that I remember the song
but not the words,
and that I've forgotten how to fly,
I wonder if one day I'll realise
that I've left it too late to dance
and I'm left crumpled
like a little fairy
too exhausted to take to the skies

I wonder what if the ice never shatters,
and the heavy sands never more shift,
or if I'll fade like petals exposed to the winter,
or be weighed down by
suffocating snowdrifts

What if I never again see my star,
or sail the seven seas,
and what if at night I lie awake
with no more dreams to comfort me

Rhiannon Owens

Once Upon a Dream

Across distance and time
Hearing you calling,
Awaking, I jump
Catch you from falling,

Has this all been a dream
Or visions from the past?
Now living in the future
In a moment everlast,

Did we truly once meet
Once upon a dream?
'Cause if I'm not mistaken
I keep thinking 'what a team',

Once upon a dream,
Had it all been agreed?
Was it I, was I the one
To provide service to 'the need'?

Ashley O'Keefe

Secret Dreams

Lying in darkness
All lights are out,
Gazing at stars
There's love to think about,
This time yesterday
He didn't exist,
Now all she can think of...
Her mind will persist,
Floating along moonbeams
Flying amongst stars,
Humming her tune
To be lost without scars,
Falling so gently
So softly to sleep,
A smile in her eyes
Secret dreams she will keep.

Ashley O'Keefe
(Inspired by Lynette Rees's book, 'The Workhouse Waif')

A Special Place

Somewhere beyond our dreams
is a place where people dance,
they dance in golden rays of sunlight,
and they dance through the darkness
while Orion beams
like a beacon through the night,

They dance in the wind and the rain,
the susurration of the wind through the leaves
is a rhythm that accompanies them
again and again,
along with the gentle murmur
of waves on calm seas,
they dance across rainbows
and the milky way,
twirling within myriad galaxies,

Beyond dreams is a place that is special,
a place where we can be free...

lean close I'll let you in on the secret,
it's a place where all are welcome...

it's the heart and soul of humanity

... and it exists within each and every one of us,
a special place for you and for me!

Rhiannon Owens

Sunken Dreams

Lost and alone
Far out to sea,
Has this all been a dream?
It's been so real to me...

A voyage of discoveries
From the very start,
Setting sail with the tide
The moon and stars in our heart,

We are castaways, unanchored,
We've cut loose, sails billowing,

We are unmoored...

Flowing on our sea of words, in an ocean of verse,
We are immersed, far from the shore,

Somewhere
'Beyond the Sea,'
On this floating world of creativity,

Lost and alone
Far out to sea,
Has this all been a dream?
It's been so real to me...

Seeking poetic lands
Travelling through time,
Experiencing the wonders
We are partners in rhyme,

We are sinking, sunk, gazing up from the seabed,
Salt in our eyes, alone, sunken words,
Sunken dreams,

We are capsized…

But above us, a path through the water gleams,
And we are buoyant, never to be sunk again,
Our words are like birds, that take to the skies,
Out of reach of the waves, mocking the tides,

And just like our words,
We rise... We fly!

Lost and alone
Far out to sea,
Has this all been a dream?
It's been so real to me…

Seeing with poetic eyes
Saccading east to west,
From the ancients to the Oscars
Our writing stands the test,

On this never-ending Odyssey
Past sea monster and siren
In this blue infinity,

So many worlds
So many lands,

But no desire to drop anchor just yet,
No yearning to dig our feet into warm sands,

Lost and alone
Far out to sea,
Has this all been a dream?
It's been so real to me…

Searching across poetic sands
Our innocence lost,
As the seasons change

With the seas, we have crossed,

Typhoons whipping up cruel, lashing waves
We are dashed against rocks
Spun in a whirlpool
Caught in a sandstorm,

Cruel grains rake our faces
Pinpricks of blood on icy skin,
Two windswept, bedraggled figures
Looking forlorn,

But we battle on like old salts
The vagaries of the weather
Cannot dampen,
Our pioneering spirits within,

Lost and alone
Far out to sea,
Has this all been a dream?
It's been so real to me…

In poetic dreams
We awake, we connect,
We gaze at the moon
In our eyes, stars reflect,

The haunting echoes of sea shanties surround
Wonders of the sea and sky all around,
Are we finally homeward bound?

Could that be land in sight?
Glimmering beneath
The magical enchantment
Of those swirling Northern Lights?

Is it time to stir from the dream…
An epic voyage,

Where nothing was ever as it seemed?

We've sailed under cloak of darkness,
Been serenaded by shooting stars,
Watched over by a silvered Moon
And planets,

Venus
Mars

And those stars will guide us back again
Should we want them to,
And in some ways dreams
Are always true,

And journeys carry on,
Staying with us till the end,

For, I've got my sea-legs now
I can hear the ocean call,
so until next time…

Bon Voyage, my friend!

Lost and alone
Far out to sea,
Has this all been a dream?
It's so real to me…

Our words are like birds, that take to the skies,
Out of reach of the waves, mocking the tides,

And just like our words,
We rise... We fly!

Rhiannon Owens & Ashley O'Keefe

Northern Lights

We stand at dusk
The Northern Lights in our eyes...

Through the ages, few have passed this way
Gazing at the wonder of the skies...

The magic goes on and on...

The North Star watches as the seasons change,
Guiding us through our journey and our dreams...

It shines and never ends...

The two of us walk as one
In our hearts we know
We just couldn't make it alone,

As the world crumbles around us
Falling into the sea,
Our dreams will remain
Forever, for you and me...

Before the darkness turns to light
And our yesterdays fade away...

We wish upon that Northern Star
Remember beyond the blue and grey...

The magic goes on and on...

The star shines through the darkest night
It's taken us on our journey through the past...

It shines and never ends...

The two of us walk as one

In our hearts we know
We just couldn't make it alone,

As the world crumbles around us
Falling into the sea,
Our dreams will remain
Forever, for you and me...

Ashley O'Keefe

Wandering Star

Gazing at the ancient wanderers
above us in the sky,
that our forefathers gazed upon too
while the stars glinted
still and silent,
a twinkle in their eye...

Some of us seek the stars
to guide us back to home,
but others were born under
wandering stars,
on eternal pilgrimage,
destined to always roam.

Rhiannon Owens
(The Ancient Greeks referred to Planets as 'wandering stars'. This poem is
also inspired by the song 'Wand'rin' Star' from the film 'Paint Your Wagon')

New Beginnings

A celestial vision
In a Winter's night sky,
Planets coming closer
As time goes by,
Two drawn together
Side-by-side,
In this great conjunction
A Christmas Star as our guide,

Within their alignment
Like a single bright star,
Jupiter and Saturn
Seen as one from afar,
Above the horizon
Illuminating the skies,
Upon the Earth's dome
New beginnings in our eyes.

Ashley O'Keefe

Starlit Nights

Gazing into the starlight
Our shining eyes reflect moonbeams
Deeply lost in the night

Transported into these dizzying heights
Dancing with you in my dreams
Gazing into the starlight

Taking sweet pleasure and erotic delight
In a thousand sensual love scenes
Deeply lost in the night

Together, taking flight
Wings spread, our smiles gleam
Gazing into the starlight

You are gallant, you are my knight
Holding me in your esteem
Deeply lost in the night

In dreams the world is bright
With you, such a joy it has been
Gazing into the starlight
Deeply lost in the night.

Rhiannon Owens

Mystical, Magical
Swirling light,
Guiding us home
A wondrous sight,

Skyward gazing
In disbelief,
Written across the sky
The names…

'Owens and O'Keefe'

DEDICATIONS

Rhiannon:

To my beautiful Taff, Nicholas.
Whenever I see you wrapping a sock around an injured bird or the like my heart just melts.
I love you so much ♥... as does Iskra, Ghost Rhys, Arachne 1 & 2, Trojan, Mr Veek, Morgan, Sergei, Magwitch, Jay... and all the rest 🐦🐦

Mum & Dad, hoping to see you both again soon. Hope you enjoy the book 📖📖 Love you. Xx

Thank you to everyone across the various Facebook groups for your positive and encouraging comments... Particularly Amanda, Carl & the Team at DPS for giving us so many opportunities to promote our work. Thank you to everyone who has supported us by buying our books and/or sharing our posts. Your input has been invaluable! 📚📚Xx

Ashley - Wow! What a dream of a journey. Book 5! This was going to be our swansong 🦢🦢... Looks like War & Peace!
Thank you so much for all of your inspiration, friendship and support... Without that I would have given up writing... You are fantastic!
Here's to RHIANNO & ASLEY 🐘🦉🐀🐀

DEDICATIONS

Ashley:

As always, I'd like to dedicate this book to all my family, here and passed.

A special thank you to my wonderful wife Helen, and my beautiful daughters Molly and Erin for all their support with my writing.

Also to my mother, my biggest fan. Hope you enjoy the book.

Thank you to everyone who supports, reads and encourages us to continue with our poetry.

Again, a big thank you to my talented writing partner Rhiannon, always an inspiration, support and friend. It truly has been a journey of dreams which I can't see coming to an end any time soon. Cheers to us on book 5, and for what is still to come.

A special thank you to: -

Lynette Rees for writing our foreword and for all her support.

Carl Butler for allowing us to include his and Rhiannon's collaboration 'In Dreams'

Also to Carl Butler and Grace O'Reilly for both reviewing our previous book.

Images from Pixabay.com or authors own.

Rhianno & Asley

Book 1
A Voyage of Poetic Discoveries

Set sail with Rhianno & Asley on a Voyage of poetic discoveries to the Moon and back with our first joint poetry collection…

Let's hope Mother Nature and the Weather are good to us before the Winter sets in:

We'll be in the company of Wolves and Angels, tipping our hats to the Supernatural, before delving into the raw emotion of Humanity; exploring Loss and Sorrow but also Love.

There'll be stories both old and new, generous helpings of Folklore and History, plus you'll get to meet a host of memorable characters along the way!

We hope you enjoy your journey with us…

We hope you enjoy Our Book.

Rhianno & Asley

Book 2
Seeking Poetic Lands

Rhianno and Asley set sail once more, seeking poetic lands with their follow-up poetry collection.

Spanning the continents from Europe, Africa and Asia to the Americas they'll travel from East to West. Strolling through the streets of Paris and Rome, marvelling at the wonders of the Egyptian deserts, soaking up the sun on the coastline of Costa Rica, and experiencing the glitz and glamour of Hollywood's golden era.

History will again come alive with vivid characters while we'll hope to survive our various encounters with the beasts, deities and rituals of Folklore and Religion. There'll be Love, Loss and Silliness too.

Our sails will proudly Fly high as we traverse through the turbulent waters of Passion, Obsession, Dreams and Nightmares ... all for the love of The Arts!

Jump aboard! Enjoy the adventure.

Rhianno & Asley

Book 3
Seeking with Poetic Eyes

With this third poetry collection Rhianno & Asley are Seeing with Poetic Eyes as they sail across ocean waves....

So many sights to behold! The dark side of humanity is exposed with Slavery, and the reality of life during Lockdown is explored... but we fight back, voices raised in Protest. Despite our Sorrow there is always the capacity to Love.

As the waves swell beneath us we journey through Ancient Times, where Vikings, Druids and female Ninjas abound. We rub shoulders with Sherlock Holmes even as the Saloon Gals of the Wild West seduce us.

Ever onward we sail, singing our Sea Shanties that tell of Shipwrecks, Selkie and Sirens.

Sail away with us...

Rhianno & Asley

Book 4
Searching Across Poetic Sands

Rhianno & Asley are Searching Across Poetic Sands in their fourth poetry collection...

Drifting past Wales there is a yearning, the Hiraeth carried on the sea breeze, but there are further adventures to be had as they delve into the murky depths of the Thames and the Penny Dreadfuls, where pestilence and death abound.

The Titanic sails past on her maiden voyage, not knowing she is swimming against a treacherous tide. We will also encounter deadly Obsession that can only end in Murder! From the turbulent seas of the Supernatural & Unexplained to the still waters of Childhood, there is something for everyone.

So many more sights to behold before we drop anchor!

Enjoy the Voyage...

Printed in Great Britain
by Amazon

79247721R00180